NEW YORK
TIME

RICHARD PECK

NEW YORK
TIME

Delacorte Press / New York

Published by
Delacorte Press
1 Dag Hammarskjold Plaza
New York, N.Y. 10017

Manufactured in the United States of America

Design by Terry Antonicelli

First printing

Library of Congress Cataloging in Publication Data

Peck, Richard.
    New York time.

    I. Title.
PS3566.E2526N48   813'.54   80-22829
ISBN 0-440-06346-9

FOR BETTY KELLY

NEW YORK
TIME

CHAPTER 1

MARRIAGES are funny things. Let me tell you about mine. First of all, I married Tom Renfrew. You may remember him yourself if you happened to go to college with us. At 6 feet 1 inch he was the shortest center in the college conference the year we lost to everybody but St. Mary's of the Woods. A catch nonetheless.

Up there in the cheering section, palpitating amid the last of the felt skirts and cinch belts, I first scouted Mr. Right dribbling down the court in the last of the crewcuts and the glasses taped to the temples.

Oh, Lord, what made us think we knew enough to commit marriage at twenty-two? And, listen, it was regarded as binding in those days. "Well, how could we?" I asked Tom. "Know enough to do a thing like that, I mean?"

I put that question to him on our fifteenth anniversary last summer. We observed it with a splurge at Chez Paul, that bogus gastronomic temple on Rush Street. It's the suburbanite's idea of a night on the town. I was the only matron in the place not in subtle yellow or lime green.

"We didn't," Tom replied, smelling a cork. It was a cork-smelling kind of evening. We'd even toyed with the idea of having a drink beforehand at Crickets.

In the prismed light he glittered a little, like a nonsuicidal Richard Cory, in his creaseless summer-weight dacron-and-wool Brooks Brothers blend. Men are the natural peacocks. I never know what to wear.

Though we don't find table talk necessary or even desirable at home, this was an occasion, so we chatted on, naming all the things we'd been innocent of on our wedding day. Day, not night. As post-Puritan midwesterners we don't talk dirty as an artform.

"Mortgage rates, of course," Tom mentioned right off.

We made an inane game of our lists that lasted right through the lemon mousse. The childless play games too, and we don't have to let anybody else win.

"Not just mortgages," I offered. *"Rent."*

Oh, I forget now the whole list. It went on and on. We hadn't yet heard about Black Power or Welcome Wagon or Alice Cooper or feminism or transactional analysis or the Shiite Moslems. And though Tom had known I couldn't cook, he hadn't known I hoped never to learn.

It turned out that there was quite a lot more that we didn't know than we knew, if you follow me. Things like Open Admissions and Endust and *impact* as a verb and gasohol and Skylab.

So all right, it won't replace backgammon; we enjoyed it. I for one was glad to be out after dark, though my feet were killing me because I'd come right from work. I hadn't become a career woman to actualize myself or to make a statement. Back in the mists of history, I'd taken a job to put Tom through his MBA. And since time flies even when you aren't having fun, I was still at it years and years later. My eye drifted repeatedly to nearby tables where my fellow females were thrusting at spinach salads with strength in reserve, having saved themselves for a strenuous evening by rising at noon to miss their exercise classes.

I was in my final stages as a sportswear buyer for the Number Two department store in Chicago, which is quite a step down from Number One. Such were our revels that we sat at the table till quarter past nine, and then I couldn't get my shoes back on swollen feet. After let's say, thirty-five, you may have some cute left, but just try to get your candle to burn at both ends.

Persons of our stripe go out of their way to avoid sloppy sentimentality. But as I rose flat-footed from the table, I was tempted to remark that possibly fifteen years of marriage was but a prelude.

Something stilled my tongue, though. I can't think what. Maybe it was the last item on Tom's list. He'd been saving it back. "Bo Derek," he breathed.

That was last summer, and I don't recall dining out since. It's winter now, in Cook County, Illinois, a season of thermal underwear and reflection.

I've been reflecting like crazy all winter. And rereading Daphne du Maurier. What a little sap that second Mrs. de Winter was. With a staff like that, I could have run Manderley *and* Maxim with my left hand.

But I was talking about reflection. I have all the time in the world for it because I've quit my job at just the age when it's chic to start one. I've walked, pensionless, away from that welter of weskits and Ship 'n Shore blouses and the regretta-

ble order of A-line skirts that wasn't moving. I have suffered
my last management trainee, fresh from Northwestern, who
mistakes a career for an elective course. And I need never
wonder again whether or not Peter Pan collars are on the
comeback trail.

I kept my nose to this grindstone till Tom's accountant
calculated that we were paying the IRS in the neighborhood
of a hundred a month plus my entire salary to keep me in the
job market. And so I'm at home. Buried half-alive in a ghetto
of well-kept hussies who have never been anywhere else.

I hardly know the house by daylight and find myself out
of focus. Years in Leisure Sportswear have killed any interest
I might have had in clothes, but they also kept me from developing any taste for household skills or the Junior League.
I sit here in the far corners of rooms, more like the second
Mrs. de Winter every minute, wondering if I ought to give a
costume ball.

For a less stable personality, this could be a winter of
marked discontent. But I look for little features that give the
day shape. The mail delivery, for example. It's erratic in
winter, but that only adds suspense. And I reflect. My mind
creeps inevitably back to early days.

Marriage. College. That sort of thing. As I've said, a marriage was performed between Tom Renfrew and me.

How we actually met I don't recall. It was senior year in
the time just before meaningful relationships flowered readily
from the passed joint. Somehow we ran the gamut of house-
mothers, a fully floodlit campus, and all the boilerplate of an
age even then on the way out. An age of innocence to be
sure, though you don't lose it all at once.

This much I do remember after better than a decade and a
half: the breathless hiatus while I waited for Tom to get over
one Isabelle Van Donder, the class nymphomaniac.

I writhe to recall how I lingered on cold nights outside her dormitory. She was of course not taken into any sorority, though she'd been taken in at any number of fraternities. How I lingered on the way home from the library, books to my camelhair bosom, dreading to catch one wrenching glimpse of physically flawless Isabelle and hardly less lovely Tom under a shrub by her dorm door in those manic moments before some bathrobed warden shot the bolt.

My brain boggled at shot bolts. But I saw nothing in those numbing nights but my own breath and never even had the satisfaction of learning anything later. For all I know, Tom may never have scored with this gynecological miracle.

It was merely the majority co-ed opinion that Isabelle left no first-string center unturned. And come spring and the baseball season, busy Isabelle had her own definition of RBIs. So I wandered past endless nocturnal topiary, limp with desire and sunk in ignorance. And I graduated still not knowing a diaphragm from a dress shield.

Or an IUD from a Q-tip. Somewhere along the way, though, Tom took my bait. Before graduation day the diamond solitaire was on my hand. In the summer after senior year, I was in ten weddings, one of them mine, and amassed a lifetime supply of dyed-to-match satin pumps with pointed toes that went out the next season.

Ours was a garden wedding in Waterloo, Iowa. My father gave me away in a driving rain, and Tom's mother handed him grudgingly to me. He has never sent out a shirt to a commercial laundry in his life.

I have the wedding pictures, though I'd prefer to remember it in my own way. I, cast as a leggier Sandra Dee, with her bubble cut, and a slight broadness in the beam all my own, legacy of too many midnight sorority taffy pulls.

And Tom, backed up by his six groomsmen—national finalists all in a Pat Boone look-alike contest. Ours was the last clean-cut collegiate generation before the apocalypse, and I

see the two of us swapping vows: a pair of sizable monu-
ments to good childhood nutrition and both a bit strapping.

At the very moment he was slipping the ring on my
finger, I was still discovering new reasons for the rightness of
this love match. The male members of the wedding party
had put up at the local motel, and Tom alone had not gotten
shit-house in the inevitable all-night bachelor party. From
where I stood, clutching white orchids and an uncut prayer
book, I could smell the evidence of straight shots on his best
man's breath. Tom's eye was clear and his breath hundred-
proof Lavoris.

And when it came his time to repeat the vows, his voice
carried manfully to the last row of sodden guests, wringing
sighs from my mother's canasta club.

I called on the weeping heavens to explain to me how I'd
landed this—this Guy Madison sent down to earth. And
with a kiss our fate was sealed.

At the Odd Fellows Hall reception we danced the ritual
first dance cheek to cheek in a circle of college pals and great-
aunts. The song was "If You Were the Only Girl in the
World." In the middle of the floor, Tom murmured, "You
are." And from my bubble cut to my T-straps I blanched
with bliss and nearly blacked out. A particularly exquisite
episode of sensory deprivation—and a hard act to follow.

We were wedded, bedded, drafted, and even graduate-
schooled before I could find the moxie to ask Tom about
Isabelle Van Donder, campus strumpet and volunteer sex
therapist.

How well I remember the scene in that little ninety-five-
dollar art-deco-and-I-didn't-even-know-it apartment in South
Evanston hard by the El. We were both in the kitchenette, a
feat in itself, and by opening the refrigerator door and pressing myself against the butter, I could trap him in the dinette
set.

By then he'd given up the paisley belts and recognition pins of college and was experimenting with an overachieving young-executive look: boldly striped English shirts with contrasting white collars, hardly patterned challis ties, and suspenders. He stopped just short of the pocket watch. Even disguised as a British civil servant, he was still the best-looking kid on the block. "Isabelle who?" he inquired in mock confusion.

Isabelle was not the kind of girl you could take the Fifth Amendment over and hope to avoid contempt of court. My gavel banged down time and again. He even tried the sleazy dodge of seeming to confuse her with Adelaide Whitehead, my roommate junior year.

But when I threatened to go for the yearbook, his eyes took on an irritating spaniel-on-a-hilltop look, though all he would say of Isabelle was that she'd been a girl of enormous spirit.

By which he couldn't have meant school spirit.

How long I was in learning what prudes men are. And how unerringly they'll squander their misplaced chivalry on all the wrong women. And how awesomely discreet they can be when it's in their own best interests. Even alone, they can close ranks. I had already spent our entire honeymoon trying to gauge the quantity and quality of Tom's experience with no criteria of my own. And had thus been lost in thought at most of the moments when I was supposed to be a real team player.

Our South Evanston kitchenette contretemps over Isabelle ended on the usual young-marrieds note. I on his lap, a little too rangy to cuddle, and he tracing the convolutions of my uninformed ear with the light brushstrokes of a mustache that was later found to clash with his crewcut and shorn off.

What brings on this sudden wallow in the past is that on this winter morning I find frozen in the mailbox, along with

the bill from Commonwealth Edison, the *Alumni Quarterly*
with the addressograph label reading *Tom and Barb* (*Blakely*)
Renfrew '65.

I never mean to read a word of it, but it's drying out on a
radiator this minute; I'm rewarming the breakfast coffee and
itching to turn to the Class Notes, which exercise some obscure hold over me. I even have my own reading routine: a
quick scan of our Class of '65 Notes, reported by our Faithful Scribe, Liz Welty Oberholtzer, to see if anybody died
and then a systematic start all the way back to the earliest
classes, lumped under *1914 & Before*, which are obituaries
all. Then I work through the eras, scrutinizing the capsu-
lated lives of perfect strangers, as in the Class of '18:

> After 62 years in the funeral direction game, Philo Lum-
> ley (BΘΠ) is enjoying retirement in his Daytona Beach
> double-wide mobile home with his lovely Hester (Gates,
> '19 ZTA). Philo and Hester welcome all news and visits
> from classmates and anybody else.

Here follow more obituaries, men and women alike dying
like flies up to the Class of '24, when the widows take over:

> Mary Grace Hobart (Rexroth, ΔZ) has embarked upon a
> whole new career—in show business (!) as a grand-
> mother-type in a TV commercial for Macro Farms
> Whole Grain Cereal. "It is basically a granola-type prod-
> uct," Mary Grace reports, "and with residuals and
> Medicare, I'm making it." Right on, Mary Grace!

There follow mainly the changing addresses of restless
relics until a reasonably interesting entry for the Class of
'29:

Wedding bells for Viola Zellbach Waggonseller Murphy (Krebs, AΦ) and Warren Potts (ΣAE). This is Viola's third marriage, all to the Class of '29. Warren's first wife, Juanita (Bullock, ΦM) passed on last year. At the Leisure World nuptials, Viola and Warren were attended by a combined twenty-two grandchildren. Way to go, Warren and Viola!

We skid then into the Depression grads, some of whom are still ambulatory and sitting on boards. And then the World War II generation, who are all either corporation presidents or married to them or lying low.

Among the births the oldest fathers are Class of '59, the oldest mothers '70.

Liz Welty Oberholtzer has next to nothing to report about our class. Somebody's daughter has won a bake-off. An old beau of mine from freshman year has just returned from a church tour of the Holy Land and reports unrest.

Apparently all the marriages are still intact, though I suspect Liz of subtle censorship.

Shortly after us, we take a dip into the counterculture. The Greek letters ebb and don't flow again until the Class of '74.

In '75 one Muffy Sturdavent reports she's into biofeedback and relaxation therapy.

Eloise (Pownell) Wilson and husband (Bruce) of '76 announce the renaming of their son Star to "Bruce, Jr." The rest of the seventies are into babies and investment banking. The class of '80 is devoted to grad school and (in a distant echo) draft resistance.

I sit back jittery from all this feverish activity and the rest of the coffee. Class Notes gets me every time, and I don't even know why.

I'm back again, the gullible ghost of the Barbie Blakely

that was, a hundred-and-thirty-pound milk-fed ash-blonde stamped out by the dozen in some laboratory of midwestern eugenics. I see me drifting among those lightly ivied walls. Cowering in queues of registration in a Brownie-knotted neck scarf. Sound asleep in chapel. Standing weak-kneed in a gaggle of terrycloth and Spoolies on the Tri-Delt balcony with Tom's Sigma Chi pin newly fixed to my shortie pajamas while all his brothers serenade all my sisters on the night of our pinning—that tentative step between nothing-doing-Saturday-night and the diamond solitaire.

Give me the Class Notes and I can evoke again a world that can hardly have been. And of course Adelaide Whitehead.

Adelaide was in my pledge class, and I hated her on sight. Everybody did, and the Actives would have kicked her butt all the way to Isabelle Van Donder's dorm except for her secret smile that promised some arcane knowledge it was thought she might be willing to share in time.

She looked (I know now) like Meryl Streep, with one faint blue vein at her temple, hair an auburn I'd have dyed for, and legs (I know now) like Ali MacGraw's.

I avoided her like a faculty tea for four semesters and then drew her as a roommate in a lottery we both lost. By then I was a totally integrated Tri-Delt, almost one of the girls except for a certain acidity I was trying to turn into irony. But by pegging me as the house clown, peer-group pressure blunted a wit I thought rapier, which I wouldn't dare unsheathe around Adelaide anyway. Her sophistication may have been forced, like forsythia, but she had cowed stronger characters than mine.

I have slipped too readily into this reverie. There are circles in which one must excuse, even confess, sorority membership. I was a sorority girl and am a wiser woman for it. In the Tri-Delt house, I learned the limits of a sisterhood's solidarity just before one begins to play for keeps. If Germaine Greer had ever been a pledge, she'd be spreading her suspicions evenly between the sexes now.

It's true, we were taught outrageously sexist lessons. Like the need to keep at least one foot on the floor when entertaining on a davenport. And how to walk downstairs in an evening gown without getting there too fast and upside down. Though I've avoided dramatic entrances since, I've always known how to walk down a flight of stairs. One day I will learn what to do when I get to the bottom.

Sorority life was not all pushing crepe paper into chicken wire and then riding atop the effect. Callow though I was and eager for approval, I would never have fallen for anything like that.

And that goes double for Adelaide Whitehead. She never learned bridge and always locked herself in her room during Hell Week. And she never ran for anything. It was a meager Tri-Delt who hadn't been elected Sweetheart of something at least once. Why, I myself was once queen of one of the lesser hops. But Adelaide remained above it all. We were half through college and she was the recognized house iconoclast before I was closeted with her. I see now the motives of the power structure: stick the clown and the iconoclast in the same room and neutralize both.

I'd expected my grades to shoot up in a semester spent with a roommate who wouldn't deign to speak to me. There had been bad pairings before, and lines chalked down the middles of bedroom floors over which neither roommate dared plant a mule.

On that first day Adelaide lolled unsmoking in the only chair while I shoved cashmere and neckerchieves into bureau drawers. I despised her ankles, thrust out across the floor.

My ankles aren't bad now, for some reason, but then I dreaded the passing of the rolled bobby socks fashion. Many a girl was snatched from oblivion by the generous folding over and over of bobby socks, those great equalizers. And evening gowns were long in those years. We in the Tri-Delta tulle shed could cover early elephantiasis by day and by night. Many an ankle was never laid bare short of the bridal bed. Adelaide's could have sold hosiery in a national ad.

"Blakely," she said to me that day, noticing that I planned to spend the semester arranging my drawers, "it's a fallacy to think that any fifty women can be friends."

I turned on her. On my left one, over the heart, my sorority pin—three diamond stars in a crescent—bristled at her. She hardly ever wore jewelry and none of it symbolic. "Don't go gung-ho on me, Blakely." Her tone was level. "A semester's a long time. Let's make the best of it."

She might have been sketching out a stretch in women's prison.

"Why did you *join?*" I whined. We were encouraged to debate things in those days.

"For three reasons," she replied.

I tried to yawn, dying to hear them.

"First"—she held up one beautifully manicured digit—"it's ostentatious not to join. I know, I know, you think the dorm's completely full of losers and religious maniacs."

I was sure of it, I thought.

"You're wrong. There are plenty of women in the dorms who have never gone through Rush out of principle. I can admire a high moral tone, but I can't live with it."

I tried for ennui, but it was out of reach.

"Second, the difference between a dorm and a sorority is the difference between a hotel and a home. The dorm's dining room is essentially a public place. You have to appear fully dressed at breakfast. I would prefer to have my morning coffee and newspaper in our dining room before I dress for the day."

I'd heard that she had an airmail subscription to *The Manchester Guardian*, and maybe it was true. And I could hardly wait for her third reason.

"Third, while there are lesbians everywhere, there's a concentration of them in the dorms and reasonably aggressive out of sheer force of numbers. I have nothing against anybody's sexual preference. But in our society lesbianism is regarded as deviant behavior. I don't choose to live in an aura of false undergraduate liberalism that's no preparation for the real world."

My hand was clutching my throat, and I seemed to be sitting suddenly in a drawer. I'd heard of lesbians and thought the last of them was Alice B. Toklas. I'd also thought Senator McCarthy had done something about all that.

In short, Adelaide Whitehead had me where she wanted me from the first day. Besides, she never barked and she never borrowed. By October I'd advanced from fear to awe. I even found myself explaining her to the rest of the girls and worrying a little about her. She was majoring in history and minoring in art without taking the Ed. courses for a teacher's certificate—which was regarded as vocational suicide unless you meant to marry money.

And she wasn't headed in that direction, because she dated an impoverished assistant professor in the art department, which was unheard of and caused the calling of a special chapter meeting to decide if it was Tri-Delt behavior.

Then one gusty November day I'd come back to the house from a zoo lab session reeking of formaldehyde to hear the TV set on in the dating parlor and the sound of muffled sobs. There were often sobs coming from there, but rarely in the early afternoon.

Avoiding trouble even then, I went on up to my room to

find Adelaide sitting in the chair, her alabaster complexion whiter than I'd ever seen it. I bustled in, always, for some reason, wanting to seem purposeful in her presence.

"You haven't heard, have you?"

I hadn't of course, not in the lab.

"Kennedy's dead."

"That can't be."

"It's true. He was shot in Dallas."

My lab notebook spilled onto the desk that wavered under my eyes. But Adelaide wasn't crying, and if I had to, I should go down to the dating parlor like everybody else.

"Not *dead*."

"Near death," she said. "They're easing us into it." And then, like the Delphic Oracle: "They'll have trouble explaining this one away." She was always a step ahead of everybody.

Feeling the world lurch, I'd planted my hands on my desk. "What will we do now?"

I waited, really wanting to know.

"That's odd," Adelaide said finally, in a new voice. "I was just wondering the same thing. We've always thought we could do anything or be anything we wanted. And now—what can we do, and what would it mean? And why in the goddamn hell try?"

I'd suspected all along that she'd meant to do something momentous, even astonishing with her life. Her every secret smile said so.

I'd already caught flashes of her future, stepping off transatlantic flights in a Jackie Kennedy pillbox with a purse like a diplomatic pouch. However hazy her achievement—something political or corporate—her future was more vivid to me than mine. I'd been sure I'd be tracked down in the end by some biographer of the first woman something or other and interviewed as a friend of her youth.

But after that day she began to change—to draw in on herself. By senior year you couldn't have picked her out of the group picture.

She never married and eventually became an interior decorator, sending Tom and me Christmas cards from Phoenix with little self-mocking notes to tell how she's cleaning up by redoing tract house family rooms. Cheap shots at herself. And on mornings like this when my guard's halfway down, I catch myself mourning the Adelaide from junior year—breathtaking and brittle and still unbowed.

CHAPTER 2

I T never fails. Nostalgia always turns me on and then turns on me. The *Alumni Quarterly* slips from my hands, Adelaide Whitehead smiles secretly once again and I invite her to go.

She was too cocksure to compromise without bitterness, and so I refuse to think of her as emblematic of our age. And yet she haunts me. I'd call her in Phoenix except it's time that divides us, not distance. And so I seek to rout her ghost by seeing her as she must be now, behind the smokescreen of seasonal greetings. Tanned to leather in her bachelorette penthouse above a desert sunset: sand-colored walls with a mannered mix of Navajo pottery and Bauhaus. A full-blooded Conservative now, with *The National Review* on her nightstand and a tax-exempt Dreyfus Fund she could buy Yuma with. And dating other people's husbands.

She'd challenged me when I'd chosen Tom for mine. We were no longer roommates by then, but by following the faint gleam of my diamond solitaire, she tracked me to the room I shared with Audrey Whipple, who fled.

After perfunctory good wishes, Adelaide asked me to explain in one sentence why I was marrying Tom without invoking either of two words: *love* or *security*.

I boggled only a little and said I was marrying my best friend. A very popular line in those days. Adelaide's look told too well she'd heard that one before and wasn't about to swallow it.

I didn't swallow it. Who could imagine one's best friend showering communally in a thicket of hairy legs? Or standing around a tapped keg listening to leering liars replay their latest trip to Terre Haute or some such red-light district? Or even singing baritone?

No, men were the great unknown and looked the better for it. But I for one wasn't going to plead for the sweetest mystery of life, not with Adelaide on my case. Or simple biological need either, which I wasn't absolutely clear on.

"So you're marrying your best friend," she echoed. "How antiseptic. But I suppose you could make it work."

I considered that I'd gotten off easy.

Growing firm with Adelaide's specter, I wave her firmly out of my kitchen. Short of a lobotomy, the only way of dealing with the past is to become one's own housemother, fully formed and heavily indulgent.

We'd all reached the age of consent just seasons before the era of viable alternatives. You either married or you didn't. I did. Adelaide didn't. Living in sin wasn't immoral; it was literary and only occurred in World Lit survey courses. And even there, D. H. Lawrence married Frieda the minute she was free. Real-life irregularities still lay in the messy future.

And we saw it coming, too—dimly. Maybe Adelaide's posture was purely defensive and mine preventive. Maybe we were both just plain scared. Possibly I married Tom as a haven against the horrors of headlines. Am I the last woman alive to opt for marriage as a snug harbor? No, there are others all around me, and more in the making. The notion is not dead that the well-chosen mate and silver pattern can bring order out of chaos, even keep the Russians out of the developing nations.

Anyway, we married.

And we were a childless couple as I've said. Early on, we'd been devout practitioners of birth control once we found out what it was. There followed a cautiously heady period when we threw caution to the winds and let nature take its course. But nature did nothing except prey on unwed adolescents.

I consulted kindly old physicians who always pronounced me potentially fecund and fit as a fiddle. And about as highly strung. I tired of being told I was too tense, inconceivably edgy.

Who isn't tense in stirrups? Whether she's rushing her fences or having her subject looked into by a family doctor with her father's face. And while I was trying to unwind and mellow with the years, they rolled by.

Tom mellowed like anything, of course. Approaching thirty when the credit card lunch had padded his peers fore and aft, he was still as lanky as a wing-tipped Tony Perkins. By then he'd subdued his stripes-and-suspenders look to unrelieved Brooks Brothers. The little pointy ends of his vest still hung loose against his girthlessness.

After thirty-five, he became just clubby enough to get a noon-hour squash court and possibly pump a little iron lest some little globule of fatty tissue cloud his horizon. I hardly dared enter the attic for fear of finding this cornbelt Dorian Gray's disfigured portrait.

After the Evanston apartment, we bought a center-hall colonial in Walden Woods, a suburb more remote. Did we still expect to expect children, or were we merely living in our investment? I forget.

Walden Woods is one of those calculated villages strung along the Northshore above Chicago, a suitable setting for those of us hungry for peace at any price. There are no political coups in Walden Woods, and if you can hack the property assessments, you can pretty well sit back and watch the rest of the world taken hostage by terrorists.

I've heard all the criticisms leveled against suburbia by the two noisiest groups: those already there and those panting to get there. And I can go along with most of their harping.

The Northshore is not nirvana. There are no stoops, and sidewalks tend to peter out unexpectedly. And when everybody subscribes to the same yard service, the overall effect is of Forest Lawn. Yes, the place is gnawingly wholesome and conformist to a fault.

But for every ageless, saluki-shaped woman in satin shorts who comes unpuffing off the bike path from Winnetka every morning, there's a hung-over booze-hound in a housecoat aiming a stationwagon down the center stripe of Sheridan Road on her morning school run.

What I'm trying to say is you can pretty well choose your life-style as long as you keep your windows decently draped and don't turn your side yard into Jonestown.

Of course the suburbs aren't for everyone, and certainly never for children. Who wants to be the mommie in charge of a sleep-over of nine-year-olds discussing designer labels all night? And how rattling to learn that while your hotshot high-schooler pulled down all As last semester, so did every other kid all the way to the Wisconsin border. But as I say, we were a childless couple.

And if grades no longer matter, addresses do. Conversationally, desirable real estate is to the childless what horrors in the public schools are to the parental. If you can't hold forth on the one topic across the brimming thimble of Amaretto, you better be able to fall back on the other.

Ice groaning on the Lake Michigan shore was clearly audible in my kitchen six months out of the year. It groaned like anything that morning. After my *Alumni Quarterly* reverie I make a pit stop at the stove, lingering over the directions on a Mrs. Smith's Deep-Dish Mince Pie that I'm baking early to take the chill off the kitchen. One of the joys of the childless is that you need not pretend to bake anything from scratch.

To make the one-inch slits in the pie, I reach for the knife and plunge it into a top crust as pale and powdered as a Barbara Cartland heroine.

The mindless blade quivers through frozen tundra. On the final slab, it jams all the way in to the hilt, leaving an intaglio of my fist in the top crust, which begins to sweat. "Do not defrost," Mrs. Smith whispers in my ear. "In God's sweet name, Do . . . Not . . . Defrost."

But my fist is in the pie, and the knife blade has vanished far into rigid minceflesh. Deep-dish indeed. The pie has acquired its own handle, which I lift to find jammed right through it like Excalibur, like *en brochette*. Right through both crusts and the foil pan.

Now I see. I've been mutilating my pie on the stove top, and my coup de grace was directly over the little hole for the pilot light, which the blade entered and plumbed. It could happen to anyone, but it's just a little more likely to happen to me. Curls of smoke rise from the tip of the knife. A smoking knife? Yet another unsolved suburban crime.

I hunker before the oven, only to hear Mrs. Smith at my ear again: "If your thermostat for indicating the correct temperature is not accurate, baking time may vary." And often does. I once baked a Dromedary instant cornbread for the entire weekend we cross-country skied at Galena. And got a new stove out of the deal.

This is no slattern speaking. You don't live in squalor in Walden Woods. I leave the kitchen standing tall. You could look up your own dress in the polish on the floor. There may be a little dust on the Cuisinart, but then I never have gotten around to reading its directions for use. We talked microwave ovens for a while too, but in every neighborhood, even Walden Woods, there's that persistent rumor about the woman on the next street who cooked her hand. I have always hoped it was Isabelle Van Donder.

Wondering idly if I can get away with El Paso Mexican dinners tonight, I issue into the wind tunnel of the front hall past the living room door, where it's thirty degrees and falling. Even the Boukhara looks brittle. We don't carpet in Walden Woods. We Boukhara. If you're thinking carpeting, you're thinking Highland Park—that is, if you're thinking white carpeting.

The Christmas cactus in the hanging pot is out of plumb. Its far fronds have reached the living room wall and appear to have frozen there.

No longer on the lookout for warm spots, I've learned to give up being a heat-seeking device and meet winter head on. Numbness is the answer. I pull on boots and the duffle coat from sophomore year.

In time, of course, I will learn how to order my days without these annoying midmorning sinking spells. I will start a mail-order business or give my life to good works or drink. Or cruise Plaza del Lago all day until I find some other out-of-synch woman as quietly confused as myself.

But until then, I can only walk it off. I pull the front door shut behind me. Muffled to the eyes, I might be Patty Hearst on the way to a branch bank. The porch pillars are glazed, as in the best scene from *Doctor Zhivago*. My eyes are tearing, but I can make out the house across the street: the mini-manse of Libby and Chuck Smallwood.

A neo-Georgian with double door beneath beaded fan-light. Williamsburg high-gloss enamel trim with brass lion's-mask knocker winking in the gray day. Small firs, heavy-headed with snow, regimented around French windows. It's more than a light dusting; yet Libby's snow looks dusted, by her own hand. Behind polished panes the curve of a Scala-mandred empire sofa peeks out behind the knife-pleated ends of velvet swags.

Their flagstone walk was shoveled before dawn, swept again later. Above heather-toned slate, the center chimney, newly tuck-pointed, emits a wisp of blue smoke. Libby may be burning potpourri in her bedroom hearth again to scent the neighborhood.

Libby has a wonderful way with even heat and dried herbs. My mind's eye, blinking with cold, catches a faint glimpse of her in patterned stockings and gored skirt in her workroom off the St. Charles kitchen, warm as toast, doing something inventive with statice.

The state religion of Walden Woods is floral arrangement; the holy relics, accent pieces; the Good Book, the Horchow catalogue. I'd break my journey across the Yukon to nowhere with a stop at Libby's, but fresh coffee would already be made and I'd be obliged to admire the blend.

On the other hand, I'm freezing out here. I steer a course where our front walk should be. Somehow I lose my way and in scaling what seems a remarkably high drift find my-self standing atop my own hedge. My arms fly out for bal-ance, and I'm a momentary Christ of the Andes. Once over the rigid privet, I plant a boot where the street should be and I'm suddenly airborne, off the ground but flailing, like an Ozark flight out of O'Hare.

I land on my coccyx in a frozen rut, already looking up at

dead branches framed by two bootheels. Paralysis sets in at once. On the other hand, it's cold in this rut, though out of the wind. And the garbage truck is due any minute. One of my duffle pegs is hanging by a thread. I'm up again and heading off to Libby's.

I know better than to use the knocker. It's already been Brassoed once today, and Brassoing it twice will put Libby off her stroke. I press the bell and somewhere deep inside the house sound the first five notes of "Climb Every Mountain."

Libby opens half the double doors. One enters quickly because there's a thermostat in the front hall that Libby is looking at instead of at me. She's in one of her twin sets, unaccented, though she wore circle pins right up through Watergate. She seems suspended like a marionette in patterned pantyhose that cut grooves in her armpits. Her skirt is gored, loden green. And she's in her little stack-heeled shoes with the fringed golfer tongues and stitched toes. "I was just—"

"Don't let me keep you."

"Alum Day today," she sighs, eyes rolling over a lambswool shoulder. We're already making for the workroom off the kitchen, and she has already noticed my dangling duffle peg. "Have you seen this?" she wonders in passing, running a dusting hand over an accent piece on the piecrust tabletop under the stairs. It's a Victorian sewing basket, hideous with beadwork. "We picked it up at the Bermondsey Market on the last London trip. I lined it in moiré and really *use* it."

This is Libby being discreet. An invitation, in fact, for me to do something as useful as sewing the duffle peg back on. While I'm wasting her time, why should I be wasting my own?

We're passing through the kitchen now over recycled brick, ducking beneath a brace of hanging brass jam pans depending from reproduced meat hooks. The cupboards groan with Calphalon. Libby's eyes dart to the Melitta, which is already scrubbed out and dried from breakfast. "Tea, instead, don't you think?"

I nod at her nape. "Any blend. Oolong, Hu Kwa, Won Hung Low. Anything."

She endures this little sally or fails to grasp it and fingers down three bottles from a long spice rack: businesslike bottles with cork stoppers and imitation parchment gummed stickers that she's labeled in copperplate. Libby always has the thyme.

She stirs a teaspoonful from each bottle into an ironstone mortar, pestling the mess lightly. With a sinking heart, I observe that to this nothing like Lipton's is being added from anything like a bag. While she's scooping the aromatic sachet into a teaball, I read the three labels much against my will. Dried Rosemary Leaves. Dried Rosemary Flowers. Dried Lavender.

I avert my eyes, which fall on the Shakeresque table with the chamfered legs and square stretchers where Libby sits to copy recipes out of *Gourmet*. I note not for the first time that her recipe box is padlocked.

She warms the regulation brown pot from Habitat. My hands are thawing in the duffle coat pockets, where they discover those little packets of Sweet 'n Low that live there, breeding on their own. But we're destined to drink this elixir with honey. Libby glances at her watch to mark the start of the five-minute steeping. "Honey with this, don't you think?" she offers mellifluously. "Come on in to the workroom while we're waiting. I'm really down to the wire this morning because this is—"

"Alum Day."

She nods. "Did I tell you, or did you see it in *Winnetka Week*?"

Score another point for Libby. She has a direct wire to

Winnetka Week. A double one in this case because the newspaper's editor of Food, Fashion & Family Fun is also an
Alum. When Libby has cramps, they put out an extra edi-
tion.

I glance around her workroom while she's already at a Formica surface giving five minutes to a permanent arrangement
of dried baby's breath taking shape in a silver punch bowl.
Pruning shears in graduated sizes range just off her right
hand. There's also a small receptacle heaped with minute
maroon velvet bows on powder-blue toothpicks. She's just
fixing the first bow into the baby's breath ball and stepping
back for aesthetic distance.

"The significance of the bows?"

"Sorority colors," she murmurs, never looking around.

But I do. Libby's workroom is a sort of clinical potting
shed. Everything from bugloss to liverwort is hanging in
dried bunches from Styrofoam beams. There's also a clump
of dyer's-broom. I recognize it in a moment because it too is
labeled. In Colonial America she'd burn as a witch on this
evidence alone. There are also dustless shelves ranked with
bottles of a size usually associated with unfortunate fetuses.

I'm avoiding the heart of the matter. Libby is chairperson
for the local alumnae cell of Pi Beta Phi sorority. I recall my
past. Libby lives hers. Nor did I misspend my youth with
her. We're guardedly friendly only because our front doors
align. And because our husbands once fell out over something to do with leaf bags, and Libby and I have wordlessly
agreed to rise above such macho posturing.

If I read the Alumnae News in *Winnetka Week* instead of
my own college's irrelevant *Alumni Quarterly*, I wouldn't be
here in Libby's workroom on Alum Day. She's embarrassed
on my behalf, and hers, because I'm not a Pi Phi. Nearly
two decades are missing from Libby's mind, and we're a pair
of freshmen at some cow college in Muddle America, and

she's just been given a bid to Pi Phi, and I've had to settle for Something Else. But has this gone to her head? Impossible.

The sane observer of this scene might wonder why Libby doesn't patronize me prettily for being a nonmother rather than a non–Pi Phi. Of course she's not childless, heavens to Betsy no. She's cloned herself twice and sent the results off to Northshore Country Day.

She's Supermom, and a full-time scourge of the PTA. But on Alum Day she abandons her children to a childishness all her own. And never once dreams of lording her fertility over me. This is not Libby's priority. Wombs are a dime a dozen, but there are never enough Pi Phis to go around.

We're sitting now in her Chippendale dining room with the Old Sturbridge floral paper. Baseboard heating whooshes over ancient, twenty-year-old hand-pegged floors. I have always thought that a perfectly appointed house was a sure sign of a marriage on the rocks. But on the evidence of this one, Libby was a grass widow the minute she set foot in the Furniture Mart.

We once had a conversation that veered near the substantive. She'd sat me down at this selfsame Henredon table, and her seamless little forehead furrowed with worry.

Straightening both candlesticks and an epergne, she finally found her voice. "Supposing you had this friend . . ." she began, ". . . and you had . . . certain . . . information that maybe—just maybe her husband was . . . seeing another— you know—woman."

I leapt to the likely conclusion that she was the friend and the straying husband was Chuck, the cipher she's married to.

"A simple case of infidelity?" I queried briskly.

Her fingertip traced woodgrain. "Suspected infidelity." Her voice was careful.

"What's your—the evidence?"

"Oh, nothing really. You know how people talk."

She seemed on the verge of tears, and I narrowly escaped clapping a hand down on hers and saying, "You poor kid," or words to that effect. But I wasn't hearing confessions that day.

"Is your—friend's husband satisfactory otherwise? A basically stable type?" Libby's Chuck is stable to the point of catatonia, so I figured we were on safe ground here.

"Oh, absolutely, a model husband." Libby spoke in a rush.

"Then I'd close my ears, shut my eyes, and conduct business as usual." (I had no doubt she could manage that.) "Screw the gossips."

She planted a little hand on her heart and heaved with relief. "Oh, good, that's what I thought too—in so many words." And then in the same breath she seemed to be describing a school tea where she was scheduled to pour, ending up in a kind of triumph with a recipe for finger sandwiches. A close call.

And we're not going to have another today. We are instead at her dining room table drinking odiferous slop out of Spode. I'm intrigued by honey that spoons effortlessly out of a Waterford pot because I always have to hack my honey out of a screw-top jar absentmindedly stored in the refrigerator.

Libby's head is bowed over her cup, either in prayer or to savor the pore-dilating steam. She's keeping her luncheon menu simple and says so, brushing a cast-iron curl off her forehead. "It's only a by-laws meeting, but we have a couple of darling new girls. One from the DePauw chapter and one from Monmouth."

Libby went to the University of Illinois, but the names of private colleges trip easily from her tongue. "We're starting out with the cold rhubarb-strawberry soup. Maybe you saw my recipe for it in *Winnetka Week*?"

Maybe.

"And then curried orange chicken, which you make ahead. My apricot nut bread. And a mousse with the crystallized violets. I went bananas crystallizing violets this year."

God help a diabetic Pi Phi, I do not say aloud.

"How do you like the tea?" she's asking.

I'm down to the dregs, or something.

"If you could get it into an aerosal can, you'd have a dynamite deodorant," I hear myself saying. There. I've gone too far.

She's remembering to tinkle a giggle, but with rue her eyes are laden. See, Barbie, they say, that's just the kind of thing that kept you out of Pi Phi.

We may be within spitting distance of the first of the hot flashes, and we're still going through Rush. Two grown women. I rise to go.

"I don't know why you don't get more active with your Delta Gamma Alums." She's trying not to hurry me out, though we can both smell curry heating up.

"Tri-Delt," I say with menace. Competitive still.

Whatever, her eyes answer as I step out into the nostril-sealing cold. At my duffle back with the icebound treadmarks I hear the distant tintinnabulation of crystallized violets beyond the closing door.

Out there in the knife-keen morning my thoughts are clarifying like Libby's butter. The blanketing snow becomes a white page on which a pattern appears. In the matter of same-sex camaraderie I have gone from Adelaide Whitehead to Libby Smallwood. Though it's taken me years, I've moved from being immoderately wowed to *tant pis*.

An epiphany occurs, and I realize that at last I've evolved in my own right, a sort of impregnable aspic, lightly spiced and fully jelled. I've been making too big a deal out of trying to get through these long mornings. After all, the chief

periods of adjustment in my life are all well behind me or far
in the future.

I am roughly midway between matriculation and the
Florida condo, between one childhood and another, between
being first laid and laid out. What, me worry? Oh, yes, I'm
perilously near self-satisfaction that morning. I hope I enjoyed it.

CHAPTER 3

THE bathroom radiator isn't even breathing heavy. A sharp wind's howling, possibly from out of the medicine cabinet. I'm stepping out of the shower at the end of the day.

Damp ringlets flash-freeze against my temples. Steam curls off my torso. Over the years, I've shed four of those hundred-and-thirty undergraduate pounds. But from where?

Search me.

I'd dry off behind the shower curtain except *Psycho* was on the other night, and like a fool I watched it again.

Gooseflesh is reacting against toweling. Still, there are compensations. My skin's taut against the elements, and my thighs, though mottled blue, have looked worse. I find I can't get a good handful of either one. I like to think that at my best I'm a Lee Remick and a half.

I reach for one of Tom's castoff robes on a hook behind the door. It's a comfort to try on something once in a while that's a mile too big. *That's an amusing little nothing*, I remark to a mythical Nieman's salesclerk at Northbrook Court. *Let's see it in a 6.*

Elbowing a circle in the ice on the bathroom window, I look across the street. A dim green light glows in the study of Libby's consort, Chuck. He's an attorney with a specialty, according to the rumor I've circulated, in the defense of brothel madams.

Upstairs, Libby's silhouetted against a bedroom window. She's either measuring for new curtains—at midnight—or dusting a valence. And she's wearing a sleeveless blouse. My nipples shrivel.

From the marriage bed I hear my own consort sleeping, audible through two walls and a walk-in closet. In my day, you didn't know a man snored until it was too late.

It's the time for more reflection. I ease myself down on the toilet lid. This is Walden Woods. If you're thinking bidets, you're thinking Glencoe, as long as you're thinking flowered porcelain. I review the day.

It was all too typical until Tom tumbled off the six thirty-five Chicago & Northwestern, stamped damp Totes all over the entry, shrugged off his Baskin's British warmer, and dropped his bombshell.

I have not come to expect the unexpected from him. And he rarely regales me with news of his career. He's middle management with either Title & Trust or Casualty & Life. I forget which. He's done seven years at each firm, and though I never forget a face, corporate morphology is in one ear and out the other with me. Besides, any woman who takes an abiding interest in her husband's work is a meddler.

His three-piece gray flannel enfolded me in mock-hungry embrace. We have grown a little ironic with one another when it comes to physical contact. Once lust has ebbed, it requires a viewpoint.

Then came the big surprise.

"Guess where we're going." There was a calculated sprite-liness in his tone I was supposed to go with.

"Out to dinner," I said hopefully. "Anywhere. Even Fanny's."

"Think bigger."

"The Bahamas. For the rest of the winter. Other people do. I'm the only white woman left in the neighborhood."

His hands tightened on my upper arms. I was to try again.

"Wait a minute," I said. "Someplace off-season, but better than here. I've got it: London for Lent."

He gave me a small terrier shake. Possibly we were nearing the end of his patience. And possibly I wasn't taking this seriously enough. Still, I sensed we were to make the game show format last.

"Going," I said thoughtfully, "as in permanently? As in sell-the-house?"

I seemed to be following his lead. And he was still clasping me so close I could only get a fix on the knot in his tie. He was holding off on eye contact. "You mean *moving*?" I verified. He seemed to be nodding.

Haven't I already mentioned that abrupt change intimidates me? "You mean packing crates and moving vans? That type thing?"

I was sure he was nodding. The tie knot was going up and down. My pulse quickened. "You've been fired."

For this piece of insensitivity, I was put at arms' length and got eye contact. The big baby-browns flashed fire. "They're calling me into the home office as a department head." His tone was direct, businesslike—aging young executive scrambling up the corporate ladder, could use a spot of support and awe from the little woman.

But I was desperately trying to remember where the home office is, if I ever knew. "Don't tell me. Omaha?"

His eyes searched the ceiling for forbearance.

It might be Hartford, Connecticut. That's a big insurance town, I think. But I didn't know how many wrong answers I was permitted. "Suppose you tell me," I said, forfeiting the game.

"New York." His gaze was unflinching, but I saw a flicker of uncertainty in the left pupil.

"It's a big state," I said, playing for time.

"New York City," he said.

Just like that. When I haven't even completely unpacked from the last move. A scant seven years. British families are famous for occupying the same moldering ruin for five hundred years at a clip. Oh, the hectic pace of modern life.

I have returned to myself on the toilet lid. My mind reels. We're leaving Walden Woods just as I've solidified my position as resident sniper, with my innocent little japes at Libby's life-style. This calls for more than a review of the day. This calls for agonizing reappraisal.

I haven't been honest with Walden Woods. I've frozen, no pun intended, into a pose. I've counteracted its smug little pieties with smug impieties smaller still. I haven't even played fair in the matter of cuisine. This very evening I didn't give way to frozen El Paso Mexican Dinners. I served up a passable arroz con pollo (though I used garlic salt) and a crisp salad for which I fried and crumbled bacon, though the Bacos gestured alluringly from their bottle the entire time. My board groaned. And I defrosted nothing but the pie I've already confessed and not merely because Tom once addressed me as Evelyn Nesbit Thaw.

It's true I won't bake. Because deep down I know that Mrs. Smith and her prissy little sidekick, Sara Lee from

Deerfield, aren't actually a couple of annoying women. I know they're enormous industrial complexes that pay union scale.

I can cook and willingly would, but all around me are a hundred Libby Smallwoods who always have the Armagnac to do *glace aux pruneaux*—and the patience. Women who can flambé in long frilly sleeves without impersonating irate Buddhist monks. An entire coven of women, and the occasional bitch of a man, who can make flowerlets out of anything, and always with a Sabatier Jeune. Persons of all sexes who make their own croutons. I have made of myself a crudity in a wilderness of crudités. I rest my case.

And speaking of rest, my bedmate and I are the only couple between here and Howard Street who do not slip nightly between Porthault sheets.

But here's the kicker. My quilted spread and, yes, the dust ruffle are Nettlecreek, bought with a store discount I no longer have. I've been half had and methinks, only in private, I doth protest maybe a little bit too much. While Libby's getting off on having been a Pi Phi during eight distant semesters, am I not just a little pointed with her about being a fallen-away Tri-Delt? And what can it matter in a desperate world?

Except that now it seems I'm about to see something of that world. And Walden Woods—too late, too late—takes on a faint little *Gemütlichkeit*. While lifeless limbs scrape the bathroom window, I feel unexpected roots being ripped from the Permafrost.

Let's look at the plus side of Northshore living now that it's too late. While we've been sheltered here seven years, the house has gone from ninety-eight five to heaven alone knows. Six figures, big ones. I'm overtaken by a small *frisson* that has nothing to do with the climate.

While our mutual fund went down the commode twice, the old real estate has jumped over the moon. All we have to do now is find an Arab Pi Phi and go into escrow.

Facing facts, I've got to admit Walden Woods has been a pretty good deal. And no Peyton Place either. To be sure, many a marriage has washed right out into Lake Michigan. And many a woman more anxious to please than myself has awakened to a note on the pillow.

But Tom and I have been proof against everything, even creeping affluence. I put it down to mutual respect and separate bathrooms.

And as we both knew at the time, I was lying to Adelaide Whitehead when I told her I was marrying my best friend. Bleaching his underwear is hardly the function of a friend. Nor does he call from work and chat for hours. And I've never tried to book him for lunch lest he opt for the squash court over me. But we're very friendly, and in his version of flippant, he's even been known to parry a thrust or two of mine.

I forget when it was that I told him I'd been unfaithful to him time and again. This barely raised his eyes above the level of the *Trib*. "Time and again," I repeated, "but of course only in my heart."

"Anybody I know?" he inquired. "Because, listen, if I can put in a good word for you, I'll—"

"You can hardly be said to move in his circles." I said this crisply.

"I give up." He turned to the sports section.

"You may as well know," I said. "It's Phil Donahue. I'd welcome that silvery little Irish thatch into my arms any old night that you care to be conveniently away on business. Believe it."

"Phil who?" Tom asked, almost looking up.

I could have sworn we'd had that conversation before.

No, life up here in never-never land has been a pretty cozy proposition. And even at my most mordant, I've never been excessive. I've never voted Democrat merely because my Republican neighbors do.

And now I'm on my feet, wrapping the bathrobe twice around me. And I'm standing at the bathroom shelves while my fingers sort washcloths with little minds of their own.

What's the point in shipping threadbare Fieldcrest wash-cloths, even at company expense, when we'll shortly be within striking distance of—what's that place called?—Bloomingdale's.

CHAPTER 4

IT snowed a foot and a half yesterday: a sure sign of spring. Seven weeks have elapsed, and we're getting systematic about the move. Authority has been delegated and guidelines laid down. It's my responsibility to sell the house, crate the china, dispose of debris, run an ad for the car, and get the yard in shape if we can find it. Tom's job is to instruct his secretary to clean out the top drawer of his desk at the office.

The van line has sent out a small spinster of a man with a clipboard; they must be saving the strapping studs for the actual move. The small spinster has felt all the furniture and told me that my chest is cracked.

I live now chiefly in the interstices of the house. High garrets where I uncover dusty memorabilia. I lose a crucial half day over old yearbooks when we're measuring in minutes now and making lists at the dinner table.

A yearbook falls open naturally to a certain page, a full view of myself, nearly a centerfold. It seems I was the Naval ROTC Queen of the Military Ball in its last functioning year, just before unknown, dovish hands torched the armory. I have already mentioned that I was the queen of one of the lesser hops, but is this the face that launched a thousand ships? And if I was the winner, who were the runners-up? Quadriplegics? Or did all the Tri-Delts dating in the Naval ROTC coerce their men to throw their votes my way in some whacky quirk of panhellenic competitiveness?

The mystery deepens as I search the picture for clues to my own identity but only learn that I was then composed entirely of clavicles and glasses. (This shot is not full-length: my ankles are cropped.) And why was I, who need glasses only to read, photographed in them? What was I reading at the time the flashbulb went—*Mutiny on the Bounty*?

It's beyond me. As I snap the book shut, I notice I was wearing a circle pin and that while the face is dimly familiar, the figure isn't. All the yearbooks go in the out pile, along with a dog-eared *Franny & Zooey* and a tall yellow and black stack of Cliff's Notes. My bridges are burning. I mean to have no more background than an Arlington Heights society leader.

I lurk more than I work up in these attics, chiefly in withdrawal from the real estate women. I've learned to shy from the click of their confident keys in the front door and their overfamiliar yoo-hooing that ululates all over the house, rattling windows.

There's much irresponsible cocktail hour twaddle that you can "turn over" a Walden Woods property by nightfall on any day you care to mention, which I fell for. All I knew about selling a house is that around here we don't plant signs in the lawn. But I thought one well-placed early-morning phone call to a realtor would result in making the new owners welcome by lunch time. I have seen this on TV time and again. It was not to be.

By lunch my kitchen was full of a real estate woman ("Call me Pearl"), swilling instant and zeroing in on the fine line above the refrigerator where I had maybe not papered quite all the way to the ceiling.

Pearl of the thunderous thighs sits with legs akimbo and "puts me in the picture." She's wearing a polyester pantsuit, so she cannot be from nearer than Niles. Yet she makes very free of herself in Walden Woods. "Well, it's not Winnetka, is it?" she points out, "but then it isn't Glencoe either."

I have to go along with this, while noticing that like the van line spinster, she carries a clipboard. The top sheet is a form on which she keeps making what look to be minus signs. "Original kitchen," she says.

I hadn't seen it in that light. Maybe with a greenhouse wall at the back and a fireplace and barn-siding cupboard doors and Libby's meathooks, you could lay claim to a little originality. . . . I murmur something modest.

"I *mean*," Pearl groans, "*the* original kitchen. You haven't done noth—anything *with* it."

Or much in it.

The rest of the house too leaves her, in every sense, cold. "Yeah, and I suppose it's *oil* heat," Pearl says. "Jesus! Don't ask any of the prospects to take off their coats. Anyhow, in here they're out of the wind. It'll *seem* warmer. And if any of them ask what your fuel bills are running, tell them you got a terrible head for figures, which you probably do. You know where I'm coming from?"

Niles, I nearly say. I nod instead. And stop trailing her in the living room which she's pacing off with Earth shoes.

Retreating to the kitchen, I struggle for a mien of frozen

dignity but only achieve the first part before she lumbers in, asking, "Whatcha want for it?"

"What's it worth?" I'm already too eager, and sound it.

"What you can get."

I mention a six-figure figure.

Pearl shoots me a look. "You been talking to the Part-lows."

The old hag's right. I've heard word of what the Partlows of Riparian Lane have just sold their place for, and I've matched them to the dollar—reckoning without the fact that their neo-Norman pile has a cobbled courtyard, suede powder rooms, a pipe organ, rentable chauffeur's quarters, and a turret suitable for tipping boiling oil down on peasants.

I come down five thousand.

"We'll be here all day," Pearl grunts.

I come down forty thousand more. Pearl's eyelids narrow. We seem to be leaving petrodollars and entering the realm of possibility. "We'll take a shot at it," she mutters, managing to imply that she alone can off-load this turkey.

Would that she could. We go from here to something called Multiple Listing, which means I hold an open house for every realtor on the Northshore. Dispiriting though it is to clean a house when the sole advantage of moving is to out-distance old dirt, I glaze the place in lemon oil and Butcher's wax. I'm not out of a crouch for three days. At midnight I'm in mobcap and kneepads whistling jingles from commercials.

There's a temporary break in the weather on open house morning as a fleet of station wagons draws up. Harpies with business cards arrive from as far off as Waukegan. They struggle to locate a path to the door, then blaze one. They hit the front porch at their top speed. The house heaves.

In some halfwit magazine I've read that a salable house needs to look both decorative and lived in. One helpful hint is to set the dining room table for dinner using all your good stuff. Libby lends me a centerpiece.

This bold stroke seems lost on the realtors, though not entirely. After they leave, on a wave of wet stretch Dynel, I'm missing a salad fork. This sends me reconnoitering all over the house. I uncover a Virginia Slim butt under a sofa pillow and an unflushed toilet. We are in business.

The picture of the house in *Winnetka Week* is a grainy postage stamp. Somehow, the photographer has unearthed unsuspected gothic qualities about the place. There's an ominous vacancy about the windows, and the climbing vines resemble fingers. It looks like the paperback cover on *The Amityville Horror*. And my six figures, set in type, look uncompromising. Yet I'm willing to be reasonable, even before the first prospects cross the threshold.

They arrive but not with Pearl. They're being led around by a realtor I seem not to have seen before, which with any luck means she isn't the one who collects salad forks. She flourishes a card regally. I've already noticed that women who sell suburban real estate divide sharply into two camps: the grand and the butch. This one is rather grand, given to standing in the dead centers of rooms with a fur-trimmed coat thrown back and hand on hip, rolling conspiratorial eyes at me while the prospects check the place out.

I refuse to believe the first pair of them will prove typical. They appear to be father and daughter, though if they are, we have a case of incest on our hands. As the grande dame and I lead them upstairs, she murmurs, "Second marriage."

I take this to mean it's *his* second marriage because *she's* obviously only in tenth grade. We're all separated in the upstairs hall, and I find myself giving the grande dame a sales pitch on the half-bath off the master bedroom. We realize that we're quite alone. I find the second marriage in the den

where *he's* giving *her* a good feeling-up against a standard
lamp. He wears bifocals and a tartan cap—indoors—which I
take to indicate baldness. And come to find out they're really
in the market for something "more gatehousey" at "under
seventy."

From then on I take up my post in the attic. When I hear a
key in the lock below, I only glance out a dormer window. If
the prospects have arrived in a Cadillac Seville or its equivalent, I drift downstairs with a half smile of wan welcome. If
not, not.

From the dormer I notice that Libby across the way is
more caught up in this daytime drama than I am. Her swags
twitch continually as she checks out the action. She too is
calculating the cars. And I suspect her of taking down license
numbers to run a make on the plates. Libby has already
implied in all kindness that if I don't sell to Really Nice People, she'll find a way to blacken my name in New York. I'm
proof against this idle threat but growing strangely sentimen-
tal about the old place and wouldn't mind seeing it in good
hands.

For days, though, all we get is a steady stream of bimbos.
Even hard at it in the attic erasing the past, I hear disconcerting scraps of dialogue echoing up. "Will they be leaving the
curtains?" in a highfalutin' voice.

"Probably not."

"Thank *God*."

As with any hunted thing, my hearing improves. Downstairs there's little dealing on the side. Somebody from out of
a Mercury Marquis asks Pearl if my Welsh dresser is for sale.
As New York evidently has no dining rooms, my ears rise to
perfect points.

But nothing doing. I hear the Welsh dresser being scraped
out across the dining room floor, and someone's discovering
the Colby's label on the back side. Another fabulous fake un-

masked. *Libby's* Welsh dresser would be imported straight from a Swansea cottage and sadly scabrous with woodworm, and she'd now be turning it over for forty-five hundred dollars.

I learn too, from very literal eavesdropping, what's negotiable and what isn't. What goes and what stays. Light fixtures stay. Washer-dryer is negotiable. Basketball hoop over garage door and compost heap stay. Radiator covers are negotiable. Radiators stay. Heat has already left. Husband goes. House stays.

Wife is negotiable.

CHAPTER 5

THE house is sold. And not, needless to say, to the father-daughter act—with any sense, they're looking in Harvey—nor to the next hundred and fifty hot prospects.

And I've had it up to here with second marriages, reformed hippies in Peugeots, grass widows in Gloria Vanderbilt jeans who are gearing down from Kenilworth, and twenty-five-year-old snotnoses in puffy parkas who look suspiciously like they have the down payment. How can you establish credit before puberty?

But the house is sold, to a very tweedy couple, though one is more tweedy than the other. They are childless, like us. And they've had the good taste not to comment upon mine, though I have followed their eyes as they silently remark certain imperfections: the slight ripple of patching plaster, the little dangling gray worm of frozen Mortite with which I gamely thought to caulk a window, the enigmatic light switches that turn nothing on. But they don't rifle my knife drawer, though from the attic I've heard those knives rattle twenty times in the past week.

No, they're discretion itself, and while I suspect them of planning to gut the place to make it livable, I'm not here to pick fights. And I've made them welcome from the first moment, mainly because they drew up in a spotless silver Jaguar from a very good year. At the end of the second visit, I court pneumonia by actually seeing them out and shaking hands all round on the front steps. We have come to a gentlemen's agreement and can now descend to lawyers.

This show of handshaking heartiness sends Libby's swags into a paroxysm. I half expect her to take a tumble out her French window and go sprawling in her drifted herbaceous border.

I close the door upon the receding Jag and fall back into the front hall, stoned with relief. I have but to look at the hall phone to make it ring. Libby's not cooling her heels: "Well, did they?" she inquires all in a rush.

"They did."

"Oh, wait till I tell Chuck!" And then unwilling to wait, the little idiot hangs up. She's left me all unknowing about the effect upon her. Have I sold to Really Nice People, according to Libby's definition? They seem nice enough to me. But of course they weren't really married. Any fool could see that. And neither of them was female.

CHAPTER 6

SOMEWHERE beneath a crust of beige snow, the crocuses are in full flower, and so we're merging into late spring. Libby is giving us a going-away party, and we're already attending it. The easiest thing about a party at the Smallwoods is getting there. Nor was it that easy, holding a gun to Tom's head all the way across the street and then whisking the small but deadly Derringer into an evening bag just as Chuck Smallwood opens both double doors in an unparalleled show of hospitality.

To honor the move, Chuck and Tom are willing to dabble in detente. Quarrels between men do not lend themselves to analysis. They have beginnings and ends but no satisfying middle parts you can get your teeth into. Bygones are becoming bygones in this altercation, though, and Chuck offers what appears to be a Smithfield ham. But since Tom shakes it, it must be a hand.

The stem of a martini glass projects from beneath Chuck's other fist. Still, he appears to have yet another hand and whole arm with which to engulf me while he slobbers a kiss down my cheek, muttering, "Barbie, baby," with understandable horniness.

Because Chuck is very tall, he has miscalculated somewhat; the arm meant to encircle my waist has instead my right breast in a death grip. But soft, this is no third hand at all. This is the hand with the martini embedded in it. Chilled gin anoints my starboard bosom. I issue into the party looking like a part-time wet nurse.

Following a smog of Arpège and Old Spice, I reach the edge of the pecky cypress and chintz living room, thronged by familiars. This is a decorous debauch. Here we swap lies, not wives, and there isn't a mantra among us. Libby is hard to find. She's curiously mouselike even in a group of her own devising. Nothing wrong with her dried arrangements, though.

Wondering how to remind the nearest fun seeker that I am one of the guests of honor, I let my mind wander lethally back to this soiree's origins.

It dates to a particularly lunatic bargain that Libby and I have tacitly struck. Since I've had the good taste not to hold a garage sale, which would bring in the Wrong Element from Evanston willing to pay spot cash for old Tupperware, Libby has been willing to go ahead with the party for which the guest list has already been drawn up and filled with people she owed anyway.

I would hold a garage sale, or even open a leather bar in the sun room, if it would discourage a Smallwood party. But I'm growing apprehensive about the whole New York business and think one last searching look at my neighbors will speed me on my way with more gusto.

There are no Swifts or Armours among us, though in the conversational buzz their names fall like gentle rain. The Partlows aren't in attendance either, because they've already moved. Otherwise, the gang's all here.

And here comes Mitzy Schmidtz, bearing down on me. She's always the first person you see at a party, and the last. Her Naugahyde face is wreathed in smiles, and a hand-loomed evening skirt is straining over cellulite.

Mitzy is the divorced chatelain of the three-story Victorian at the corner with the attached geodesic gazebo. Ever the neighborhood character, she hit her peak in the late 1960s. She's Oberlin, Class of '44, but she didn't come really alive until the Tet Offensive, when she ran a small halfway house for Canadian-bound draft dodgers out of her rumpus room. Having made her statement, she's still in possession of a life-size poster of Huey Newton and an angry scar under her ear where a drugged pacifist tried to kill her with her own Sabatier Jeune.

Robbed of her cause, she has degenerated into diffuse diction designed to unsettle. She's before me now, blotting out the room. "Your tit's all wet," she roars. "Want another drink?" She holds out a hardly touched frozen daiquiri garnished with a crystallized violet.

I pass it up as she knocks it back and edges me into a ficus. "So you're off to New York," she thunders, "and you've sold to a couple of fags!" She beams with approval.

At last somebody has said it. But at the top of her lungs. I seem to go deaf. Or the room has gone silent. "Maybe I will have a drink," I squeak. "Where's the bar?" It's probably just off the kitchen where the architect put it, but Mitzy offers to play barmaid—typecasting—and takes my order.

"Diet-Rite," I mumble and plunge deeper into the room to be hard to find. At most parties there's a dead spot in the middle, at the eye of the storm. I can usually find it. Or else it forms around me. At Libby's it's the size of a mass grave. Just as I get there, Tom elbows past.

"Let's get the hell out of here as soon as we can," he mutters.

I am not deceived. Husbands are always ready to leave parties at nine and never at midnight. Before I can take up my solitary post, he's in a huddle with Harvey Starbuck, Bob Heinlein, and Leo MacArdle, all deep into slam dunks and the upcoming Sox opener at Comiskey Park.

I'm huddled in a windbreak of upholstered backs against gusts of conversations replaying the horrors of public high schools. ". . . coach maced at Evanston during halftime . . . remedial reading now at New Trier East . . . driver-training teacher at Glenbrook South brutally tire-ironed . . ." Headlines shriek the crimes of other people's children above the tinkle of ice and shush of taffeta skirts from Trooping the Color.

This is the preferable part of every party, the early moments when it's perfectly cast with dress extras and everybody's still in character, like movies before Altman.

It's the time when you can ask yourself unanswerable questions without the annoyance of response. Such as why does everybody but me have a cleaning woman, and why are they still complaining?

The peculiar acoustical properties of this room permit me to hear whole phrases of Tom's conversation wafting from his huddle. Start eavesdropping on your husband's conversation and you'll end up having him professionally shadowed on business trips.

Still, I listen. And what I hear I like. Harvey and Bob and Leo are drawing him out about the move. Harvey's an up-

tight little egomaniac with a family business, Bob's a derma-
tologist with a Rolls named *Eczema*, and Leo's a big cheese at
Kraft. Set for life, they're a little rattled by the price we got
for the house. And they have the usual Chicago view of New
York: that it's both beneath their consideration and out of
their reach.

This is Tom's time to overcompensate with a little mild
swaggering. But he passes it up. I'm mildly curious to know
just how this transfer came about myself. We have not talked
it to death. Marriage is not a forensic society. And two people married as long as we who are still communicating in
paragraphs are either compulsive chatterboxes or of extremely southern European extraction.

It seems we're going to New York because we'll never
see—let's say, thirty-five again. All the young bloods in
Tom's company are too concerned with something called the
Quality of Life to go and live in this sinkhole. New York is
the punishing reward for never making demands on your su-
periors regarding ten-minute commutes to country clubs,
court time, and year-round blue-water fishing. It seems a
whole new generation is abroad who will gladly leap off the
corporate ladder the minute the surf's up. This leaves a certain vacuum in the upper reaches of middle management.
Evidently in New York there's a vacuum you could park the
Hindenburg in.

So Tom, who could translate *department head* into *vice-
president with prospects* and carry it off, does nothing of the
kind. He styles the whole thing as a generational accident. I
like humility in a man. You don't find it in a woman.

But now the huddle's bad-mouthing the younger generation and lamenting the decline of the work ethic, so I drift
out of my dead spot and make for a wall. This is stage two in
my partying. I'm not here for instant rapport.

En route to my niche, I come up against Marlene Millsap,

still crumbly from a facial. Her hair has had a recent, violent frosting, and a once voluptuous figure has been packed under pressure into a two-piece pink shantung. The bows on her pumps proclaim mendaciously that she's a Northshore native.

"Greenwich?" she wonders aloud, cocking a partial eyebrow. "New Canaan? Westchester, of course—Bedford Village, Pound Ridge? Scarsdale?"

Stymied by conversation made up of place names, I wait her out. Marlene has been on the move for more years than she cares to admit, riding the coattails of her husband, Hube, who's something peripatetic in earth-moving machinery.

While he labored in Houston, she put down roots in River Oaks. And for the San Francisco move, she decided on Hillsborough. And Oakville for Toronto. And LaDue for St. Louis. And Newport Beach for L.A. And Chagrin Falls for Cleveland. As a result, she's up on suburbs and the only woman in the room who knows more geography than the route to Old Orchard.

I haven't studied a map of greater New York, and so I am at a disadvantage, which is where I'm meant to be. Pound Ridge sounds like a particularly fibrous loaf of health bread, which I do not say. And I thought Scarsdale was a diet. I'm also obscurely irritated by Marlene's limiting of locales to select gatherings of the self-appointed best people. She started out in Berwyn, and I try to remind her of this with my eyes.

"Let me make up a list of the right towns for you and Tom," Marlene's saying, "Connecticut, Westchester, just the two that will do in New Jersey, and stick it in the mail."

Stick it, I do not say to Marlene, smiling and nodding at some nonexistent person over her shoulder.

Behind a shepherdess lamp near my intended hideout I encounter a perfect stranger framed by a bookshelf. A browser, she's just running an idle finger over the spine of *The Total Woman* at the end of the row of Catherine Marshalls. Except for a normally formed mouth, she looks a little like Liza Minnelli. And except for Libby's imprints, Heidi and Kimberly, who are passing canapés in long peach skirts from Betty's of Winnetka, this girl is clearly the youngest person in the room.

The obscenely young have gone back to wearing nearly real clothes again. Army issue is long gone, punk is passé, and a new form of camouflage has infiltrated the land. The example before me is wearing, apart from a training bra, a very nicely flounced wool gauze above cone-heeled sandles.

I give her a frank once-over. With the grotesquely young there's usually something self-parodying about this new costume: a gimcrack 1940s clip dangling from a limp lapel, ankle socks under ankle straps—something like that. This doll, though, is playing it straight.

But is she carrying it off? Were those size-four feet now so strapped and stilted not recently in cowboy boots? Was that cleavage not but lately restrained beneath a Bee Gees tee shirt? And would I not be in a better frame of mind if she wasn't making me feel fifty instead of, let's say, thirty-five?

"You've got to be Mrs. Renfrew."

Whenever I hear that, I whirl around fearing to find my mother-in-law looming behind me. She's been dead these many years, but she's capable of anything.

And how can this girl know me? Be not misled; some of the young are quite conscious. "You've just got to be. You're just like Mrs. Smallwood described you."

Mrs. Renfrew. Mrs. Smallwood. It's like the goddamn Colonial Dames. "Oh, call me—"

"Barbie! May I?"

Barbara is what I had in mind, but let that pass.

It seems that this perky squirt, name of Andrea, and her

husband, Wally—Wally?—are newcomers to the community. She's on the way in, and I'm on the way out, and this is our slender bond. "Getting back to Mrs. Smallwood, just how did she describe me, exactly?" I ask.

Andrea goes coy, would tuck a curl in her mouth if she weren't so thoroughly Sassooned. "Oh, you know. Like really . . . sophisticated. And . . . you know . . . brittle."

Cast into some unsuitably hard and haglike role, I simmer silently, and I *would* be wearing black too, which the cretinous clerk at Handmore assured me was simple and yet said it.

"Of course, to Mrs. Smallwood," I say, "Dolly Parton is sophisticated and Julie Andrews is brittle."

"Outrageous," says Andrea approvingly. "I knew it was you."

You can't confuse the young; they have only one idea at a time. After this rocky beginning we settle down to her life story. At her age, it can hardly be longer than a haiku.

It seems that after college she shared an apartment in Carl Sandburg with two chums of her own sex. Then—coy again—she moved out of there and into a cozier nest on Oak Street with Wally. I take this to be in a premarital state, and I'm right. Andrea says, "Really, can you imagine tying yourself down to marriage without living together first?"

If I try very hard I can.

"Oh! I bet you and Mr. Renfrew went sort of right to marriage. Right?"

Though I shouldn't, I begin to speak: "Since Tom and I hail from the era of Playtex girdles and lover's nuts, at least one of us went to the bridal bed a technical virgin."

Brittle, brittle. And true.

Andrea blinks, remembers to laugh. It's an embryonic echo of Libby's humorless tinkle. Andrea will do all right here.

But where here? Why were she and Wally not hot prospects for our house? Or were they? Is this snip the one who saw through my reproduced Welsh dresser?

Evidently not, because she's asking about our house. We skirt the party, and I give her a view of it through Libby's French window. Night-shadowed, it bulks out of the snow like a bunker on the Eastern Front. I've left the bathroom light on, and I've already taken down the curtains. The crack in the shade is obvious from here. One shutter seems to have gone askew. And it all looks cold. I wouldn't give you thirty-two five for it—furnished. Andrea declares it "cute" and opines that we've probably outgrown it.

Ah, the rising expectations of the young. I've just about located her and Wally in one of those subtly sordid apartments with Murphy bed and drop-down ironing board above a store on Green Bay Road: Walden Woods' Tudor response to the cold-water flat. After all, they are childless, of course—no sooner off the skateboard than on the pill. But I must know. "And where are you living?"

She manages to stop admiring our house. "Oh, we're in the Partlows' place."

My brow beetles. "The chauffeur's quarters? Over the garage?"

Andrea looks annoyed. As to a child, she explains, "No, we bought the Partlows' place."

All of it. The Partlows' place. My resisting mind skims across its moat, the cobbled courtyard. The French walnut paneling rising up the oval stairwell. Those marble mantels raped from Tuscan villas. The pantry you could subdivide. That difficult-to-decorate pipe organ. The asking price. The selling price. "Quick," I say, "point out your husband."

But I'm scanning the room already. Surely a second marriage. Bound to be. My eyes are skinned for some paunchy sport gamely facing up to prostatitis and midlife crisis. "Oh, there's Wally." Andrea points an unerring finger. Wally's lounged before the hearth holding in thrall Marlene Millsap. She looks suddenly and deeply in love. And *he* is evidently telling *her* about suitable neighborhoods.

His houndstooth hacking jacket from some varsity shop is turned back at the cuffs over hairless wrists. His button-down Oxford blue is knotted subtly with a regimental stripe. The overall ensemble is a sly spoof of what the big boys wear. His reddish mop ends in abbreviated sideburns, for he's beardless, cherubic. No more than a recent community college dropout, surely. His skin has barely cleared up. "What does he want to do when he grows up?" I inquire of Andrea, but her eyes are elsewhere. We're finally getting a little action at this party, and it's centered on new arrivals. Libby pops out of her crowd and coos over a pair of late entries.

A sleek twosome, and it's hard to know which one Libby admires more. They endure her with grace and scan the room with confident, curious eyes. They're the new owners of the Renfrew place, emerged creaseless from their silver Jaguar.

Busy every minute, Libby has gotten their names and number direct from the real estate office. This is a welcoming party as well as a farewell; Libby can split two for one, like a stock. She's clinging to all four immaculate sleeves: the pin-striped pair and the tweed.

"What a dynamite pair of dudes," Andrea breathes. "Are they—"

But Mitzy is upon us, a glass of colorless liquid held high. She's walking slowly backwards through the party, fixated upon the newcomers. Her chins sway ruminatively; she'd expected something more along the lines of matching jumpsuits and glitter along the eyelids, possibly lacy underwear peeping over black rubber.

Libby is drawing them more deeply into the party. She'll be procuring Pi Phis for them soon and urging them to settle down.

"Is that gin?" I inquire of Mitzy.

"You said Diet-Rite."

"*Now* I say gin."

Good-bye, Walden Woods, good-bye. I have never mastered the subtlety of your nuances. It's time to go, and we will as soon as I rescue Tom, whom Marlene Millsap is holding prisoner against a hutch. I'm off to a more elemental landscape than this one, and a simpler life. New York, here I come.

CHAPTER 7

NEW YORK by all means. But am I ready for it? Will it have Crate & Barrel and Fanny Mays?

In all my Leisure Sportswear days, I avoided buying trips to Manhattan, so all I know of it derives from our high school senior trip. And all I recall is the Dixie Hotel and the round hole under the doorknob where the lock should have been. And the ratlike bellhop who tried to sell us oregano. I know too that when the Smallwoods went East for a vacation, Libby liked Williamsburg better.

And it's time to get serious because I'm already on an eastbound flight and will arrive before Tom's worked the car out of O'Hare traffic.

I haven't flown since the flight attendants underwent sex changes. A large, bumbling, randomly barbered boy in a tailored shirt has just fumbled a plastic cheese board with bruised fruit and tightly sealed Monterey Jack into my lap.

I'm soloing on this flight because I've been sent on in advance to find quarters. Tom has stayed behind for the closing and to take a firm hand with the movers.

We could live at company expense in a New York hotel room for up to ninety days while we locate a new nest, but the thought of three months of street traffic from without blending with snoring from within has sent me scuttling on ahead to make short work of the housing business, which most people make far too much of.

I crumb my front and start up the aisle vaguely in search of guidance.

Why is it that the only magazines on planes are *Black Enterprise* and *Scientific American*? From the empty seat beside a dozing businessman I filch yesterday's *New York Times Magazine*. He also has the latest copy of *New York*, but he can keep that; I'm fighting clinical depression as it is.

I regain my seat as the near-somnolent drawl of the captain pipes in that we're six miles over Uniontown, Pennsylvania. I leaf through the magazine to the back, past the convertible sofa outlet ads to "Luxury Homes and Estates."

The offerings omit city life as sedulously as Marlene Millsap's conversation. And it seems that everybody on the eastern seaboard has his/her own Har-Tru tennis court. My eye lingers over a gaudy offering in Mamaroneck, wherever that is, with waterfront, heart-shaped indoor hot tub, and lavish built-ins at $42,000. I resort to my glasses and find that the figure is the annual rent on a two-year lease.

The flight attendants are closing up the bar and sending drunken Babbitts back up the aisle. I have had two empty seats beside me, but this is too good to last. A flabby dipso in a waffle-piqué polyester leisure suit accented with ball points collapses in the aisle seat too near me.

He can't remember where he'd been sitting nor, probably, the flight's destination. I avert my eyes, but I've got a talker on my hands. He's leaning my way.

"Say, honey, you one of them career girls?"

Can you believe it? I give him the look that withers. His sideburns reach down to his chins. One word from me, of any sort, and I'm committed.

But he only thinks I'm hard of hearing. "Businesswoman, I oughtta say, ha ha. Businessperson, I better say, ha ha ha. You wanna know sumpin? You're the only woman on this whole friggin' airplane!" His sausage fingers are fumbling my way across the drop-down middle seat. A lodge ring glitters nearer my knee.

"I meanta say, sweetheart," he booms, "pretty little thing like you don't go in for a career." He breathes heavily on me, and my right eye tears. "Do ya?"

I clear my throat. Oh, yes, I am about to speak. "I am an interior designer," I explain to this pathetic W. C. Fields. "From Phoenix. I've parlayed a resale number into a listing on the Big Board. You know the Big Board, buster?"

He blinks. It's possible he wasn't as drunk as he wished to appear. His hand is in a holding pattern.

"You a family man?" I ask. "Homeowner?" And his bloated hand goes to his breast pocket where there is inevitably a wallet pillow-shaped with laminated family snaps.

I wave a stagy hand. "Spare me the Polaroids."

"Say, listen—"

"No, sweetheart, you listen," I cut in (what's come over me?). "You're from some wide place in the road—downstate Illinois, Indiana, right?"

He withdraws his hand, palm down, fearing that I've been reading it.

"You live in a raised ranch you bought as a shell and Sheetrocked it yourself, right? Your idea of interior design is a paint sale at K mart. You went for indoor-outdoor carpeting on the family room. Correct me if I'm wrong."

His face pales to lavender. His hands hang loosely between his own knees. He's spelling out the in-flight magazine in the pocket before him. But it's too late for pity.

"Plastic birdbath?" I suggest. "Checkerboard panels on the garage door?"

I'm feeling really quite ballsy out here in the world. Haven't been off my turf in a coon's age, and I can handle all comers. I've seen articles in *Redbook* about how women are fighting back these days, but I had no idea it worked.

I even permit myself to think it's going to work in New York. We're losing altitude now, and the beamish boy flight attendant is leaning across Leisure Suit and picking cheese foil and grape stems off my lap. We dip into cloud cover looking for Newark.

Newark? Yes. I'm creeping up on New York by degrees. And I've foresworn even a night in a midtown hotel. Instead, I've sent the old bucket down the long well of memory and come up with Sue-Jo Pennypacker. Sue-Jo Pennypacker Russo as she is currently styled.

I guess I'm edgier than I admit if I've had to dig up Sue-Jo. We haven't set eyes on each other since she was withdrawn suddenly from the last year of high school, short of the senior trip. At about the same time Billy Gillespie was hastily dispatched to Kemper Military Academy. But I've followed her fortunes in a general way over the years, enough to know that she's married to somebody other than Billy Gillespie and lives in Tenafly, New Jersey. I've even ferreted out her address and invited myself to stay with her during my house hunting.

We break through low-hanging clouds over a surly expanse of dirty brick. The plane must have overshot America, and now we're sweeping in over some dour Iron Curtain country.

We're setting down now, startling a flock of Cessnas. A company Lear jet swerves out of our runway, and the pilot, white with shock, gives us the finger. We have arrived.

Leisure Suit, cold sober, is the first one off the plane.

There's nobody remotely like Sue-Jo Pennypacker in the terminal. I let my luggage go around for three revolutions. Still, I am unclaimed. Every woman in the airport looks like either Gilda Radner or Shelley Winters.

As I'm thinking of having her paged, a tremulous voice sounds behind me. "Bubbles?" I *knew* I shouldn't have dredged up high school.

I turn to a perfect stranger. In fringed leather pants tucked above Charles Jourdan boots. She's flipping a Gucci key ring in a mesh driving-gloved hand. I chance a look at her face.

There, flanked between heavy gold loops that turn her ears into handles, is the ghostly visage of Sue-Jo Pennypacker. The poverty-pinched face of youth has been erased and restored by dieting. "Bubbles?" Her lips form a half-hearable question as she considers trying somebody more likely.

"Sue-Jo Pennypacker."

"Bubbles Blakely," she says in a far-down-the-throat midwestern moan. Her eyes fill.

New Jersey is the last outpost of the silver-foil powder room. Sue-Jo's foil wallpaper has an overpattern of fake-velvet cattails in royal blue. On the john with pantyhose rolled to the knee, I catch disconcerting glimpses of myself hunched amid the blue bullrushes of a surrealistic duckblind. There's a chandelier with plastic prisms inside the shower enclosure, and the soaps are in amusing shapes.

I've never been in a split-level house with seven levels. And I've fallen heavily twice. Once on the three steps up to the guest room level, and once on a roller skate that I rode all the way down to the family room. It was a skate belonging to

Little Renee, and I have every reason to believe she planted it there for Aunt Bubbles to bust her buns on.

I must remember that I invited myself.

The dining room is mirrored on three sides, and the guest room ceiling is mirrored too. I awake with starts throughout the night, thinking a middle-aged woman has leapt from a high building and is about to land on me.

The door to Sue-Jo and Matty's bedroom has been left open, revealing a dim glimpse of black satin sheets and a variety of candles puddled in saucers.

Sue-Jo runs orange juice through a blender and brings it frothing into my bedroom, which is incendiary with morning light filtered through bright orange Austrian blinds.

She's sent Little Renee off to school and is ready for a chat. She settles onto the bed and my foot. Her hair's tucked behind her ears, a wan nod toward suburban chic that reminds me of the first day I spotted her in fourth grade, the only kid with a lunch bucket.

"How did you sleep?"

Hardly at all. For one thing, the house is floodlit on all four sides, and the glare's terrific even through the metal mesh mysteriously covering the windows. Besides, I spent half the night walking my dinner through tangled shag. It was ziti, boiled potatoes, commercial coleslaw, onion rolls and blueberry muffins, Jell-O in a shape.

Lightly challenged regarding her table manners, Little Renee upturned her hot fudge sundae on the plastic lace tablecloth, and then bit her thumb in the direction of her father in a curiously Mediterranean gesture.

"And what do you think of Matty?" Sue-Jo prudently skirts Little Renee in favor of her father.

It's hard to know what to make of Matty, though I'm beginning to have my suspicions. A squat, swarthy character with a neck projecting from his sternum, he seems to be moving at high speed even while seated at the dinner table. He wore boldly stitched tailored denim and what seemed rosary beads draped across hairy cleavage. "A prince," I tell Sue-Jo.

She sighs. "He was a godsend to me, I can tell you. After you know what happened in senior year. . . ."

We observe a silence for her youth lost in an unwed mothers' shelter. Her firstborn is nowhere in sight and must be someone else's family member. No, by God, it's grown by now. Sue-Jo and I look bleak for differing reasons.

"Well, after *that*," Sue-Jo continues, "I didn't even have a high school diploma *or* a baby. I'd given them *both* up. And I couldn't go back to *Waterloo*. So I knocked around a while and then got a job as a stew with the airlines. A feeder line."

"Without a high school diploma?"

Sue-Jo plucks at her peignoir. "That's the really funny part," she says, meekly sly. "I did it sort of incognito. I used your name, so when they sent back to school for my records, they got yours. That's what's so funny about you turning up after all these years. It was always like a bond between us, and now here you are. I always thought of you as my best friend."

Oh, Lord. But, yes, there was always someone in high school you barely knew who thought you were her best friend. Very few such people, though, make use of your transcript.

"You got such wonderful grades in English," Sue-Jo says, "I was always afraid the airline would notice. I kept my mouth shut all I could. Then when I met Matty and came East, everything was fine. People never listen to you out here."

And Matty is no English major either. "He adores you," I say, shooting in the dark.

"He really does," Sue-Jo sighs. "These people are crazy about blondes." I suddenly notice she is.

Even before coffee, the day begins to dawn on me. Sue-Jo has waited twenty years for a friend to visit, and here I am. She'll bar the door if I give her half a chance. The windows have already been secured in advance. I have to take a firm hand with her in order to get up and dress.

She intercepts me in the living room, where I'm vainly looking for a morning paper in an expanse of white velvet, white shag, and white acoustical tile. There are red glass pendants on the lamps, and the modular seating is paved in plastic. Sue-Jo rushes in lest I make a bid for freedom through the picture window.

She leads me into breakfast. The coffee is Medaglia d'Oro but weak as tea; her life seems evenly divided between Iowa and Sicily. I sit at the table confronting Cream of Wheat and cheese Danishes, while Sue-Jo sits opposite, admiring me.

It's hard to be admired at breakfast unless you're on your honeymoon. In the gold-veined wall mirrors, I can see dozens of her all the way to the floor. She's wearing Lily Pulitzer jeans. Around her neck is a silk scarf knotted at both ends, plus an Elsa Peretti silver bean which she fingers. We have already run through our girlhood memories.

"Tell me about your husband." Sue-Jo tries to bend her bean.

Husbands are never around when you need them. If Tom were here, she would be admiring him. On the other hand, if Tom were here, we'd have left at first light. "Is he dark?" she asks, priming my pump.

"Gray," I say. "Crew cut." She sighs and turns a six-carat diamond on her finger. And taller than I am, I do not say, kindly.

"And you have no children," she murmurs in open envy. We are both savoring little Renee's school day.

Turning the conversation to the morning's business, I mention going to New York. She counters with Riverside Square, which must be a nearby shopping mall. I point out that I'm not going to New York to shop. I hear myself saying that I'm going to look for a place to live. In New York— City.

Sue-Jo's eyes go out of focus. "Live? In New York? Nobody does, do they?"

"Where did Matty grow up?" I fire this zinger right between her eyes.

She smiles as if she has me. "The Old Neighborhood."

"The what?"

"The Old Neighborhood. That's what he always calls it."

"Well, that's surely New York, Sue-Jo."

She tries to pleat the plastic lace tablecloth between thumb and finger. "Is it? I never thought."

I feel the day ebbing, along with my resolve. It occurs to me that I don't know where New York City is from here, and Sue-Jo's not telling, if she knows. She's talking Tenafly a mile a minute. She even offers to get out the white-on-white Mark VI and tool me all over to sell me on the place. But I have the distinct impression that Tenafly is not on Marlene Millsap's list of The Only Two Towns in New Jersey That Will Do. And I'm right. When I can get to my purse, I check Marlene's list and the two towns are Peapack and Far Hills, which sound remote. And I'm already as far from civilization as I ever mean to be.

On the way out the kitchen door, we trip a burglar alarm. She deactivates it with a single panicked swipe. "Come on. Let's get out of here. Matty *goes crazy* when I trip that thing by mistake."

"Matty? How is he going to know?"

"It rings at his office too. Come on, get in the car. We only have a couple minutes, tops."

The Mark VI is by Bill Blass, with Garden State plates reading MATTY-JO. She does the right thing to silence a siren attached to the garage door, and we roll backwards into the morning.

She's gunning to the corner when we're passed by a tinted-glass Cadillac limo bristling with bruisers. Sue-Jo and I watch in matching rearview mirrors as the limo plows directly across her lawn, and figures in big black suits peal out of it, taking aim at the house. Sue-Jo negotiates the corner and floorboards the Mark VI.

"What business is Matty in, Sue-Jo?"

Little Renee's baby shoes on a ribbon sway nervously over the dash. The Gucci key chain quivers in the ignition. "He's in zippers."

Over last night's ziti he also mentioned in broad terms an interest in restaurant napery, a school bus franchise, something called "disco concessions," and a congressman. I settle back not knowing whether I'm in deadly peril or whether I've never been safer in my life. Sue-Jo shows me Tenafly.

There's something here for every taste. The usual brace of half-timbered Jacobeans. Two or three Puritan saltboxes garnished with Mercedeses. A whole regiment of cast-iron hitching-post boys in whiteface. Six or eight Taras with rainbow trim. An awful lot of concrete Venus de Milos in circles of pachysandra. And enough electrified fencing to put Solzhenitsyn in his place.

"Oh, Bubbles," Sue-Jo burbles hours later, "I think you could be as happy here as I am."

I think she's about right.

We're home in time for little Renee. She stalks in from school in Wedgies and glitter socks. For her eighth birthday she's been given an ear piercing. Tiny crucifixes depend from inflamed lobes. She snaps small fingers at her mother, who leaps toward the kitchen in search of Tang and a plate of Stella d'Oros.

"You staying another night?" Little Renee turns on me and props a pudgy hand on her little hip.

"Possibly one more."

"Christ!" says little Renee, stumping off to her suite.

At dinner (lasagne and corn dodgers) Matty lectures me on Tenafly real estate, gathering his stubby fingertips into bunches and thrusting them into the air for emphasis. He turns a Hallmark napkin into a town map and draws lines with a fork to illustrate the frontiers between black neighborhoods and white.

And I'm not to worry about the mortgage business because they know him at the bank. "Hey," he says, raising shoulders and palms, "what's money? Am I right? You don't even need the bank. I can put you in touch with people."

Little Renee is asked not to spoon corn relish onto her cut-velvet chair seat. She responds by reaching far across the table and flipping her father's glass of Giacobazzi onto the rug. While her mother sponges it up, I withdraw to a distant phone and call Tom.

"What do you mean, she's married to a hit man?" His voice wavers in from Walden Woods. But I can't talk louder or repeat. The house is full of extensions. In a sort of verbal shorthand I tell him that if it's all the same to him, I'll give up on the suburbs.

He wonders how many suburbs I've seen in a day.

"One," I say loud and clear.

A whole new life-style is forming frantically in my mind. "I'm going in to New York tomorrow," I tell him, "if I can find it, and buy an apartment. A co-op, or whatever they're called."

There's static on the line, and doubtless we're being moni-
tored by people in satin ties from the Old Neighborhood.
Tom seems to be saying that it will require several months to
find the right thing.

I explain that I'm only going to buy one apartment, not a
whole building. Still, he says, still and all . . .

"Look," I whisper hoarsely, "I'll buy the first apartment I
see, okay?" He seems to be laughing merrily, and he's no
merry laugher as a rule. The static takes over.

"I mean it," I tell everybody on the line, "the first apartment I see."

When will I be home?

"Tomorrow night," I yell, throwing caution to the winds.
"No later."

I return to the dining room and dessert (spumoni and
Twinkies).

CHAPTER 8

NEW YORK is a place where you're continually addressed as *lady* by people who've never met one.

I've heard it three times in my search for the A train platform: from a token seller, a transit cop, and an outright derelict. I'm on the platform now, a mile underground at the George Washington Bridge station, waiting for the train, or something, to come out of a hole. Astride my suitcase and gripping a *Times* bought upstairs, I'm thinking of Sue-Jo.

With grief and foreboding, she drove me to the New Jersey side of the bridge, where I caught a bus into town. Never fated to make a clean break, I sat with her in the Mark VI waiting for the bus and picked endless lint off my skirt.

Because I've packed my traps, she thinks I've deserted her

in favor of a hotel. In vain I explain again that I'm going to snap up an apartment, grab a late lunch, and head for the airport, any airport. I may have to live the rest of my life on the East Coast, but I'm not going to live the rest of the day here.

Matty has told Sue-Jo that nobody can find an apartment in a day. And she believes everything she has ever been told, except for what I have told her several times. Her eyes are filling again, as in the days when she was never chosen hall monitor. She's working up to telling me how much my transcript and I have always meant to her. Her mind is straying back to the thousand petty, cruel, memorable little social distinctions of early adolescence that kept us apart then as the bus pulls up finally, parting us now. "At least call me from the hotel," she says in a broken voice.

I lean across little Renee's dangling bootees and give her a quick hug. She buries her face in her hands.

Loosely coupled subway cars explode into the station. Some of the doors bang back, and people flee out in what may be terror. To make sure this thing is really public transportation, I search the middle car for some identifying mark and read instead an airbrushed announcement, in puce:

TYRONE GONNA CUT YO FACE, MUTHUH

This must be the train.

Just past the 125th Street station it grinds to a halt. Bottles in brown bags skitter down the aisle. People grunt softly and scoot leg over leg along the plastic seats. The lights dim. We're there for twenty minutes, but nobody says a word, and what do I know? I fish a small flashlight out of my bag and play it on the *Times* real estate classified.

Cooperative apartments have their own section. The print is minute, but the superlatives know no bounds. And the whole thing is in code. I'm not letter-perfect in this language. WBFP, which crops up a lot, has me buffaloed. I pull out a felt-tip to work farfetched acrostics in the margins, considering everything from *Wide Board Front Parlor* to *Wet Bar Finely Paneled*.

The flashlight battery goes dead, but the train leaps forward, lights blazing, and we're off again. I've come near the end of the co-op listings. All the half-million-dollar offers and everything that needs a TCH of RNVTION or LOVING HNDS I X out. The page begins to look like a love letter from a Stephens College freshman. And I repeatedly confuse the monthly maintenance fees for the sales prices.

There's a final offer, at the end of the last column. And this one will be it. I've run out of paper, and the day isn't getting any younger, and the A train is hellbent.

For added drama, my hand covers the last apartment. As we flash past the catacombs of the Museum of Natural History, I uncover my new abode:

> BY OF AL TMS
> PRE-WR CHRM
> LV U BRTHLSS
> STUPEN VUS
> COMPT GOURMKIT
> OVSZ BDRM
> WBFP
>
> ! WN'T LST!

"Eureka," I remark to a fellow passenger, a woman who's been edging nearer since the blackout. Too late I notice both her feet are encased in Godiva Chocolate shopping bags bound at the ankles with Christmas ribbon. Her hat is cork bottlecap liners crocheted together.

"Praise Jesus on yore knees!" she replies, toothless and with conviction.

We rumble into the Columbus Circle station, which is probably quite convenient. I hustle my suitcase to the door and issue through as Lady Godiva calls after me, "Keep yoresef clean, for He is coming. You can make book on it."

I rise at random to the street level and think I may have overshot mid-Manhattan. Nearly all of New York looks like the south end of the Loop.

Working through a crowd gathering in advance of an accident, I hail a taxi. Green as a gourd, I get right in without scrutinizing the driver. I'm in, suitcase and all, before I see through the bulletproof divider the name under his identifying picture. It's in the Cyrillic alphabet. The photograph itself is a nightmare: a trained bear in a cap.

He turns this hardly human head and growls, accusingly, "I watch you come out of subway."

I'm amazed, even moved, to have been noticed.

His English is buried beneath some foreign accent, but he's clear as anything. "You one dipshit of a woman go in subway. You want rape? You want . . ." His great paws leap off the steering wheel and strangle the air. He has not thought of shifting out of neutral. I have not thought what I'm doing in this cab. The traffic backs up, blaring behind us.

Lapsing into his own tongue, he's still telling the dashboard what a dipshit woman I am to go into subway. Innocent still, I scan the sidewalk for police. The cabby's regarding me over the hump of his shoulder. Even through blurred bulletproof, I descry madness in his eyes and a lot of hair growing out of his ear. I am on my own in this situation. I take measures.

Edging up to the divider, I'm nearly nose to snout with him. "Say, listen," I howl, "where are you from anyway?"

He seems taken aback. "Sheepshead Bay. Brooklyn."
I weigh this against his accent and take a flyer: "Before that."
"Minsk."
"You mean Russia?"
He nods firmly.
"I thought you people couldn't get out of that country."
He looks canny, presses a thumb into his cheek, which probably speaks volumes in Minsk. "Is better there," he growls.
"Then why don't you go back?"
Or why don't I just get out of this stationary cab?
His thumb and forefinger massage each other in the universal dollar sign. "I save up. I buy Chevy Caprice. I *go* back!" he yells. "In Minsk you wanna know what they do wit muggers, hookers? Labor camp! Every sonabitchin' one! Decent woman *go* in subway in Minsk. Come out fine."
"*Is* there a subway in Minsk?" (Another shot in the dark.)
"Is building," he grunts. "You wanna take subway where you go now? Get outta cab and take."
"*You* will take me where I'm going." I settle back, adrenaline coursing through me. You've got to take a strong stand with creeping communism. Look at Carter.
"How I take you someplace? Dipshit woman give no address, don't know her—"
I bark out the real estate agent's address. "And I know where it is," I add, firing another burst of bravado. The cab leaps ahead, scattering pedestrians all the way, to an address in the East Sixties, which I take for an urban renewal site in very early stages. I've never considered any neighborhood desirable if the garbage is removed from the front. Stalin is warming toward me within his limits, and wondering aloud if I'd like to buy a Fabergé egg. We draw up abruptly enough for my head to hit the divider. He reaches over and

plants a paw on the meter. He can reach any distance. "Is double fare because we cross Fifth Avenue."

That green I'm not. I appear to be poking in my purse, but I'm actually working my suitcase to the door. I'm out and in the gutter and hear myself screaming, I who haven't raised my voice since I was cut from the pep squad. "Russians is one dipshit people!" My voice echoes ungrammatically down a grim brownstone canyon.

He's climbing out on his side, preparing to come around and do to me what he undoubtedly did to Prague.

I retreat a step, directly onto the foot of a meter maid who's at curbside, drinking in this drama. His gaze shifts from me to her. The sight of a woman in uniform seems to stir ancestral misgivings in him. He retracts into the cab in slow motion and guns off down the block.

The meter maid extracts her foot from under mine. Her perky uniform cap is cocked atop countless corn rows. "Whooooeeeee," she remarks, "you got a mouf on you, you know what I'm sayin'?"

I nod, agreeable to anything.

"What he *do*?"

"He tried to charge me double for crossing Fifth Avenue."

"Shoot!" Her gold and white smile radiates. "You chicken-shittin' me?"

I assure her that I'm not.

"That's one I ain't heard. What you pay him?"

Suddenly I remember. "Nothing."

"Nuffin!" She bangs her book of unwritten tickets against a jutting hip.

"Nuf-thing."

"Girl," she says, "you better get yore white ass off the street. He gonna come around the block and pound the piss outta you, you know what I'm sayin'?"

How could I fail to? The next thing I remember clearly is

issuing into a parlor floor office called "Hillary Howell for Exclusives in Brownstones & Cooperatives." I've never been so glad to be anywhere in my life.

Hillary is just turning sloe-eyed from a bay window where she's witnessed my street-theater performance. Her body rhythms are immensely languorous, but the sight of me adds angst to her Weltschmerz.

"Can I help you?" Her whinny is mail-order finishing school, but it's the first line of standard English I've heard all morning. "It seems you've had a little trouble." Her head gestures toward the window. She keeps a desk between us.

"I don't know if you'd call it trouble here. I've been accosted by a religious nut on the A train, held up by a Soviet cab driver, and a black woman just called me 'girl.' "

"Coffee?"

"No. She was darker than that. More mahogany."

"I mean," says Hillary, "would you like some coffee."

Hillary knows a nut case when she sees one. She has the glazed inward look of one who's had a spot of analysis herself. I settle into the client's chair and try to impersonate sanity, which the minute you think of it is out of the question.

She moves, pelvis first, toward the coffee urn. She's been wrapped by Diane Von Furstenberg, and her bosom is as pendulous as Catherine Deneuve's. She's wound around with diamonds by the yard, in broad daylight, and appears to have had a comb-out on a speeding subway train.

"What did you have in . . . mind?"

I rattle the real estate section and tell her I'm interested in the BY OF AL TMS that will LV U BRTHLSS with its STUPEN VUS, its WBFP, its COMPT GOURMKIT, and its OVSZ BDRM. And I hope it's still available because I'm told it WN'T LST.

It won't, Hillary assures me, which means it has. She

sidles back and extends a cup. What one hears about the killing pace of New York doesn't obtain with Hillary. Even to get her moving, I decide against telling her I mean to buy this apartment unless it turns out to be in Staten Island.

Hillary consults a mental checklist. "Empty nester?"

I beg her pardon. She explains. I look indignant—*am* indignant at the suggestion that I might have grown children. (Never mind that business about Sue-Jo Pennypacker; that was in *high school*.) I also look gimlet-eyed at the single parent query. We establish that I'm neither single nor a parent. Hillary nods with guarded approval. (She can't shake that initial impression of me raving in the street.) But it seems I'm answering right because the co-op's board likes neither children nor singles.

That we've just sold a property and are in a position to buy another is one more star in my crown, but the name Walden Woods rings no bells with Hillary. Neither, I should imagine, would Chicago.

I relax, unable to hurry her along, and in time she wonders if "both our energy is up" for looking at the apartment. We're finally out on the sidewalk, heading, I assume, to the BY OF AL TMS. Hillary mentions again and again that it's located in the "Katharine Hepburn general area."

Though what we're walking through now looks more like the Thelma Ritter Memorial Neighborhood to me. But I repeat—what do I know? Hillary jaywalks with her own peculiar self-possession across a lightly paved avenue yellow with cabs. I follow the sway of her generous hips as she defies death before bumper after bumper.

We draw up short in front of the glazed white brick of what must be a charity hospital. The lobby is black-and-white lozenges of simulated marble. "I thought we'd just have a tiny peek at this one," she mentions, mealymouthed to herself, "as long as we happened to be passing."

Obviously I'm not to be allowed to play out my plan. Hillary will decide exactly how many apartments we are to look at. She hasn't seen this one herself, she says, and I'm going to get a "very special preview before the official listing." Perhaps she's quicker than she seems.

After a hushed word with the doorman, we rise in the elevator. Wind howls down the shaft, and there is something oddly ominous, even sepulchral, about this whole business. The elevator shaft is hissing a warning at me, something on the order of *flee! flee! while there is yet time*. I can't make head or tail of it.

The building seems to be an example of 1950's luxury, New York style. Picture windows in flaked wooden frames, splintered quarter-inch parquet, main hallways only wide enough for the odd piece of Danish modern.

The elevator opens to a police blockade. Ropes bar the way down the hall, and NYPD signs caution us not to enter upon the scene of a crime.

I wouldn't dream of it, but Hillary hikes her skirts and throws a heavy leg over the cordon. I am clearly meant to do the same, and like a dummy I do. "Don't touch anything," she seems to be saying. "They'll be dusting for prints."

Far down the forbidden hall, light falls from an open apartment door. I've dropped back a prudent pace or two by the time Hillary thrusts her head inside. Her frozen half smile fades, and she turns on me, hissing, "That bitch from Hearth & Highrise got here first. She's showing the place, but don't worry about her. She couldn't sell food stamps in Bushwick."

We issue into somebody's vestibule. Sinking into a Persian prayer rug, I notice the wall paneling inside is linenfold and several hundred years older than the building. A very small, very original Corot hangs just at eye level.

The bitch from Hearth & Highrise is indeed showing the

drawing room to a very small African chieftain in a splendid gray flannel double-breasted. She is addressing him as Your Excellency, and one gathers he knows where to find mortgage money.

But the drawing room can wait. Hillary hustles me into the dining room as if we are quite alone. The paneling in here is no later than George III, and the refectory tabletop, ringed by the mug marks of Knights Templar, is littered with priceless early Meissen. The picture window has been subdivided into diamond panes behind ancient damask. The only two pieces in the room not of museum quality are Hillary and me.

At our backs His Excellency is giggling politely at the bitch. We edge toward them, staking out our claim to one corner of the drawing room, dominated by a cinnabar-red and black lacquered cabinet that is, I see in an Adam mirror, one of a pair. I hope I'm not expected to buy this place furnished, because if I am, I'm going to have to make an indecent proposal to David Rockefeller.

But Hillary finds it psychologically impossible to remain in the same room with her old enemy, the bitch, who turns enormous rose-colored lenses upon us as we pass. "Goddamn ambulance chaser," she remarks in an undertone to Hillary, never losing her smile.

"Fucking vulture," Hillary replies, curt but pleasant.

We issue down a corridor ranked with Rembrandt sketches and an achingly beautiful Mary Cassatt. The bathroom rather outclasses the rest of the place. The shower stall is gold-plated, and there is malachite where one expects Formica. The floor is from Pompeii.

"The asking price?" I ask Hillary in all humility.

But she's examining the contour of her painted mouth in the mirrored wall behind the gold dolphin spigots. Her attitude suggests that I've jumped the gun in an especially crass manner.

"Central air, of course," she says, gliding past me, "and I think a den." Across the hall she throws open *trompe l'oeil* double doors.

A den indeed. Coffered ceilings, tapestried walls dimly highlighted by bronze torchères, a trestle table to serve as a desk and possibly early Dutch, and on the David Hicks carpet a dead body.

Hillary is in the room before she spots it. She staggers once and does an about-face, thrusting me backward into the hall.

But I've seen it, in one surrealistic glimpse. My wrist is against my mouth and I'm staggering back across a Sarouk hall runner and screaming into my Seiko. I've never seen a dead body before, and certainly not one outlined in chalk on a David Hicks. The body was wearing a monogrammed bathrobe and a pair of horn-rims with a bullet hole in one. lens. He is beyond help, and so, of course, is the carpet.

This can't be happening to me, I think. But then that's what he probably thought too. I'd be crumpling now except Hillary has me by the shoulders and seems to be saying, all in a rush, "Very good north light in there, and you can see the bridge. Personally I prefer a high floor."

Through the open double doors behind her, I see another door bang open. The whole cast of *Barney Miller* seems to be bursting out of a half-bath.

The chief, with shoulder holster and clipboard, sees us huddled out in the hall. He rips out an oath, vaults the body, and bears down on us. My mind whirls. Of course he'll think we did it. And I'm nine hundred miles from my lawyer. I have the right to remain si—

"Oh for Chrissakes," he says as Hillary turns to him and I

cower into the small of her back. He's the tired New York cop of popular fiction. "Not you again, Hillary. Would you let the body cool for once?"

Hillary draws herself up. She's raddled, but this is nothing new. "This is a *very* desirable property, Malone. I want names and I want them now. Lawyer. Next of kin. Probable heir—"

"Out, Hillary." Officer Malone flaps a hand. I'm peering at him around her bust. "Now."

We're escorted from the scene as a sheet is dropped over the deceased.

At the elevator we meet stretcher-bearers and a CBS camera crew. At street level I hyperventilate and fight the urge to throw up in the gutter. Hillary is strolling now, insanely calm.

"But how did you *know*?" I wail at her.

Her empty eyes widen. "It was on *News at Noon*," she says. And since my breath is coming in short, sharp sobs, she calms me by remarking, "Listen, if it weren't for divorce, and . . . ah . . . sudden death, there really wouldn't be enough turnover to keep me in business. And it wasn't really a first-rate address. They had some hassles going co-op, and the building security isn't what it should be."

It's occurring to her by now that she might as well show me the BY OF AL TMS next, while I'm still in shock. I find the wrinkled clipping in my purse and shake it at her. "Of course," she says. "We're practically there."

And soon we are. It is the BY OF AL TMS; I'd know it anywhere. And at least it isn't in white lavatory brick or cordoned off.

Even from the street it's clearly a place where Rosemary's baby could grow to manhood without exciting comment. Fourteen floors of blackened stone rise into the brazen haze above a pigeon-splattered canopy, snapping in tatters.

"My God," I breathe at this fresh horror, "the Castle of Otranto." Which Hillary takes as approbation.

The motif here is medieval: pointed Gothic and griffins. One of the griffins, in a doorman's uniform, detaches itself from the façade and opens the front door for us. At the sight of Hillary he breaks into hideous, silent laughter. The lobby's been lavishly decorated by Vlad the Impaler.

We move out of the glare of low-wattage bulbs shaded with stretched skin to the elevator. This badly adapted dumbwaiter will accommodate one person or two double amputees. It's already occupied by a woman the size of the Grand Tetons in a floor-length mink. She's going nowhere until we get in. A carpet slipper peeping out from beneath mink is jamming the door open. Thinking I've already seen everything this morning, I have another think coming. She's nearing ninety, with brute strength to spare.

"I am waiting," she says in an awesome baritone. "And I do not have all day."

Hillary plunges into the only space there is. I follow. We're like three cats in a sack. I reach for a steadying wall and feel fur. Hillary's diamonds-by-the-yard festoon us all. Only the vast matron in mink is tall enough to breathe. She has already pressed our floor. "Another browser for 6B," she intones. "I am 5B, but I will see you up." She's looking at me over Hillary's head, which seems wrenched at an odd angle. "We are very quiet here," she booms. Hillary and I are as mice.

"The building is not what it was," she continues, putting me in the picture. "Both porters are Puerto Rican."

Hillary and the elevator shudder.

"Don't concern yourself about being approved by the board. They will take anybody these days. And have."

Hillary fetches up a little sob.

The elevator quakes to a stop. The door rolls back, and I pop out backwards, like a breach birth. Hillary follows. "Offer them half," my neighbor-to-be advises. Her mink falls open, from throat to floor. She is massively, undulatingly nude beneath. Puckered and tucked and tufted and—I should have saved the word till now—pendulous beyond belief. "I was only out a moment to the mailbox," she explains with the grandeur of Sybil Thorndike. The door closes upon her.

Hillary represses the rage that lies so near the female realtor's surface. Even her loosely wrapped breasts look put upon and cantankerous. She jerks a key in a lock and the BY OF AL TMS unfolds before us, in perfect contrast to our previous stop. It appears to be a pair of medium-sized piano crates opening off a phone booth. With a surfeit of charity, I'm willing to regard the phone booth as a foyer, but Hillary calls it "the gallery" and points out the possibility of entertaining at intimate dinner parties in it.

Just as the ad has foreseen, I'm left BRTHLSS, but Hillary manages to pry a living room window open. The STUPEN VUS are both of a Pepsi-Cola sign across a turgid river. The room itself is far less scenic. The walls are in decorator gold mysteriously splattered in rust brown, obviously from some failed attempt to swing a cat in here. Is there an unbloodstained apartment in this town?

The COMPT GOURMKIT is a pullman unit behind a rattan screen. COMPT to a fault, but GOURM? I picture Julia Child on her knees. The dwarf refrigerator is in pocked enamel instead of fine paneling, but I mistake the whole layout for the WB—the wet bar. Challenged on this point, Hillary lets her eyes slide farther out of focus.

"Wet bar, finely paneled?" she echoes.

"W," I explain, "BFP."

She snickers tensely. "That's wood-burning fireplace."

Her gesture indicates a Gothic-arched mousehole along the baseboard beside the fire door at the far end of the living room, though nothing is very far in this apartment.

The OVSZ BDRM will just about take a sleeper sofa, undistended. I foresee our modest Boukhara in here, half unrolled. The bathroom, brassbound and all in crazed white tile, is old enough to have returned to fashion. People are paying big money for wood-grained toilet seats. Having lost my taste for malachite and gold faucets, I admire the basic integrity of its pre-High Tech exposed pipes and contrast it all favorably with Sue-Jo's flocked facility, though it smells funny.

As I may have mentioned, I don't have all day. And I certainly wouldn't want to spend more of it in any place I've seen. "I'll take it," I tell Hillary.

She permits herself a triumphant titter, but she looks tired. My emotional ups and downs have worn her out. First that screaming in the street and then I nearly faint at my first sight of a little blood. We clinch the deal, but she never lets me get between her and the door.

I'm back at O'Hare before nightfall. And Tom's right there at the gate. He gives me an embrace with one arm while the other fends off a cultist selling inspirational literature.

"Oi," I tell Tom, "such a day I've had."

CHAPTER
9

THE end of August already, and
the less said about dog-days New
York the better. Through long
nights the chronically unemployed stand beneath the windows of the taxpaying, serenading us with reggae from top-
of-the-line portable radios, many of them ours.

Culture of any other sort has fled to Tanglewood, Sara-
toga, Jacob's Pillow, the Westbury Music Fair. The Beach
Boys are at the Yale Bowl.

As for the human comedy of the streets, it's a perpetual
Gong Show of people who carry their cigarette packs in their
T-shirt sleeves, numbers runners with nylons on their heads,
a lot of very minor Bianca Jaggers in splashy floral prints,
and Japanese businessmen palming massage parlor brochures
without breaking their small strides.

And yes, I'm predictably nostalgic now for the lambent ambiance of Chicago's Northshore, where the daddies stroll to the prestigious nine-forty train in crushless seersucker. And moms in divided denim, pastel tops, and very thin gold bracelets aglimmer in the iridescent noons hose down BMWs on smooth brick bordered in waxy begonias. And teen-aged children in knife-pleated tennis whites lie motionlessly convalescent in hammocks after the college boards. God bless America. I miss it.

But six floors above a sidewalk continuously piddled by dripping air-conditioners, the durable, adaptable Renfrew marriage is compressing into a couple of rooms with a minimum of fuss. Nearly past the running-into-each-other stage, we've cast lots for closet space, like Club Med roommates, and have learned which floor's incinerator room yields the best literature.

Tom's grown downright blasé. Or at least even more laconic than usual. At the cocktail hour he no longer quotes subway graffiti. And he seems to have forgotten all about the bosky dells and his-and-hers bathrooms of Walden Woods. Men are more portable—mutable heirs to a long tradition of overrunning hostile territory.

And with the sleight of hand of his sex, he's insinuated our double bed into the OVSZ BDRM, though to do it he had to rehang the door to open out into the foyer, where it doubledoors the hall closet. On the way to that closet I have opened one door and flattened my face on the next.

And why even bother to mention it—the co-op's board of directors loved him. Credit check apart, he reeks of fiscal responsibility. On Hillary's advice, I clammed up during the interview and we were home free. Standards here aren't what you've heard. You're one of The Right People, even Our Sort, if you can refrain from playing a sitar on a street corner and begging with a bowl.

There's a roof garden here at the Castle, wedged between the parapets and the water tower, and it's our new tradition to go up every evening with the six ice cubes our refrigerator can manage at one time. And there we sit in gritty deck chairs swilling Lillet and looking down on the sad architecture—like an endless Muscovite Olympic Village—and watching the sun set ultimately into Illinois.

Our conversation grows even more desultory than before.

"There's something vaguely déjà vu about this whole experience," I remark.

"I don't remember anything similar," Tom says, ducking a pigeon.

"I think it must be like that time in the army."

Tom glances over the parapet. "I don't know. It's bad down there, but it's not Fort Sill."

He'd gone from ROTC right into active service, second lieutenant. And just as Vietnam was hotting up, lucky old Tom was posted to Oklahoma for his whole hitch. I followed in a flurry of wedding-present waffle irons to play house with him in a converted motel.

"At least now we don't have to share a kitchen," he offers.

"No, but in Oklahoma it was a whole kitchen." I am ready to shift the subject further from my cooking.

"You were a terrible officer's wife," Tom reminisces aimlessly. "You nearly got us court-martialed. I could still be doing bad time in Leavenworth."

It's true of course. I was hopeless, never knowing the difference between a captain and a colonel, and their wives minded terribly.

"If the balloon goes up again," Tom says, "I could always reactivate the old commission."

"What balloon?"

"Another war. I think I'd go."

"You? Me? We could barely occupy Oklahoma. And don't

make me a war widow at my time of life. Besides, are you willing to give your life for a country that includes New York? Make the world safe for Loehmann's?"

He considers this. "At least on Saturday nights we had the Officers' Club." He gazes blindly toward Oklahoma.

It has come to this: nostalgia for bingo night with regular army rednecks in Lawton.

Though the tar roof returns the day's full store of heat, we're faithful to our aerie. Ours is not an apartment to linger in. There are no long walks in it, and when you flop down in attitudes of repose, your head and feet strike opposing walls. We sold most of our furniture to Libby, who accurately foresaw the likelihood of a last-minute garage sale after all.

But the pseudo-Welsh dresser has made the trip, wonderfully aged by the movers, who tied it behind the van and dragged it the length of Route 80. Chosen for its ideal proportions for someplace else, it dominates one whole wall of the New York living room like the *Andrea Doria* come at last to port.

We haven't brought much else. A loveseat that now looks massively modular. A tilt-top table that drops down for dining. A scaled-down bergère chair from a bedroom to keep the loveseat company, two folding chairs, and a TV tray. The effect is of Colleen Moore's dollhouse turned slum.

So I've been forced out into the mean streets in the heat of the day. Along the way I've picked up no end of street smarts: that you can beat a crosstown bus on foot unless you're in a walker. That the Pottery Barn is a pale but passable substitute for Crate & Barrel. That the try-on room at Alexander's is no place for the prim. That all those fresh-faced, wholesome girls walking Lexington Avenue aren't. And that in asking directions, you do well to omit such terms as *north* and *south*. The locals lack the Midwesterner's congenital compass.

These are only scattershot samplings of a broader education. And I've learned my hard little lessons from hard little teachers: the half-evolved transsexuals clerking at Bloomingdale's, the female Stokely Carmichaels at the post office stamps window, the Elsa Lanchester look-alikes on the counter at Mary Elizabeth's.

And I've been driven far afield from our neighborhood for stimuli and necessities alike. About the only shops nearby are those that do nail wrapping and the kind of florist that features a single tiger lily in an imari bowl. Unless these are staples in your book, you have to keep walking. And as for the supermarkets, they all seem to be the commissaries of retreating armies. You buy what they have. I've built whole meals around chick peas.

The bitterest pill of all is that all those characters by Brueghel who stalked through that first day in a frenzy of crocheted bottletops, diamonds by the yard, gapping mink, and hair in the ears—that bunch turns out to be your standard New Yorker, and this includes the dead body on the floor. Whatever happened to Kitty Carlisle?

Until this steamy night when we're about to scale new social heights. The upper echelon of Tom's firm is migrating back from their summer addresses, and somebody of the vice-presidential class is giving a dinner party.

It's eight in the evening, and the cab is heading up Park Avenue. I'm reflecting pleasantly on all those vintage movie scenes set in the back seats of New York taxis.

Our cab seems recycled from Tijuana, which only focuses my fantasies the more upon 1930s buttoned interiors. I turn toward Tom, half expecting Melvyn Douglas, and Tom's already leaning toward me. We hit a pothole hard. He takes my hand and murmurs low, "Let's get the hell out of this party as early as possible."

I am not deceived.

After a long run of green, we're brought up short at a red light behind a Porsche at the corner of 73rd. A gaggle of legally immune juveniles caper like early Bavarian woodcuts from the center island and pelt the car with sizable rocks. Deafened by this cannonade, its driver kills the engine; the Porsche lurches and stalls. Our cabby sighs, reverses, and swings around him. I'm too old a hand now to glance back to see if the Warriors have dragged the Porsche man out and battered him into a more egalitarian world.

The cab draws up beside an untattered canopy, and I'm handed out of a car for the first time since my father's funeral. Blazing with chandeliers and silvery with bleached boiserie, the lobby gives me momentary pause. Maybe if I'd spend just a day or so more at my co-op shopping . . . Still, our apartment's purchase price matched what we got for the house to the dollar, and a piece of this palace might have run somewhat more.

We rise in an elevator that has an Empire sofa in it, and I wonder what grandeur lies above. About the only tip I've picked up about New York interior decoration is that Christmas cards are wedged into venetian blinds and left there year round.

And as usual, I've waited till now to have second thoughts about couture. There's little middle ground in my wardrobe; everything's either in shreds or the tags aren't off. But since my round is not of hectic merrymaking, and Egon Von Fürstenberg has never called when I am in, the black chiffon of Libby's party is making only its second trip out into company. I reason with myself that we're in yet another transitional season and black chiffon should carry itself off, and me along with it.

The elevator is making a stately progress, time enough for Tom to send me terse telepathic telegrams in the marital mode: *Be good* (stop) *And if you can't be good, be quiet* (stop).

That sort of thing. I smooth the back of his coat collar and pick a very small thread off his shoulder. The elevator doors part.

We emerge, not into a public hall, but directly into the apartment: the ultimate status, and even I know it. The party is afoot and limping all around us. And even before my chronic party aphasia sets in, I see that this is no Halston hoedown. The black chiffon is fine; sack cloth and ashes would pass.

Set against their husbands' club ties, the wives are, to a woman, wearing the evening skirts that saw them through their last Dartmouth winter carnival. Their taste knows no season, or anything else. Silk blouses with bows drooping in unison top off their skirts by Maurice of Mt. Holyoke. A stern reminder that WASPs are an ethnic group too.

Strangers still, we whoop it up through a half glass of Harvey's and a quarter pound of Boursin biblically divided among a multitude of fourteen. Then we're somehow at the dinner table, being weighed and found wanting by somebody's Pilgrim ancestors staring down from once-gilt frames.

Opposite me sits someone whose main conversational gambit is that his Harvard roommate took Teddy Kennedy's Spanish exam. And on the wall above him, Cotton Mather. We're not here to enjoy ourselves, as the cuisine is about to point out.

And I can't make out the honchos from the underlings. I have barely spotted the host and hostess. He's the one in the club tie, and she's the one in the silk blouse with the bow, or maybe . . .

". . . finding New York?"

The graven image beside me has thought of a question. I look him in the horn-rims. "New York's whole is smaller than the sum of its parts," I remark.

There's a pause I might have predicted, and he tries again: "Have you found a place to live?"

The first course is before us, an exceedingly clear soup, perhaps drained from the eaves.

"We're crashing at the UN Towers with Truman Capote," I explain, reasonable as anything, and make a little gesture with one hand, "only until we find just the right place."

The acoustics in this place rival Libby's living room. From far down the table Tom catches my eye in fair warning.

"Capote?" my dinner partner ponders. "Is he in Accounting?"

"He is past accounting," I murmur, lowering my eyes to the Phi Beta Kappa key that swings just free of his fly.

The female on my partner's far side mutters a little something in his other ear. He rounds on me. "Oh, I see. Ha ha."

We're now being served seven peas each and something gray over rice. My chum has taken refuge in his other dinner partner, and my other dinner partner has taken note. I'm free to monitor the table at large.

What we have here is the end product of the Wharton School of Business crossed once too often with the Junior League. This is the last roundup of a great tradition. The men speak through the pinched mouths of forefathers offering legal counsel to James J. Hill. The women speak straight from the jaw against all anatomical odds.

We seem not even to be in New York. I put us around Quincy, Mass. The talk apportions evenly between confiscatory taxation, children at Choate, and something more sensational that I take to be the gang rape of some woman everybody but me knows.

But no. I have a lot to learn. Come to find out, this Sharon everybody's talking about is a Connecticut village where Our Sort weekend. But now it's being violated by the New Yorkers, who are driving its prices up and its tone down. Since we around this sumptuous board are not the New Yorkers in question, who are? This question I do not ask, for which I want full credit.

Dessert comes. A petit four apiece.

The evening ends with a whimper. In the social hour that follows our gourmandizing, the dead spot around me expands to the four walls. I consider refuge inside the window seat. At last we take our leave, shaking all hands firmly—the Yale Lock. And I only think this evening is over.

Home again, and we breeze past the griffin doorman who speaks only Aramaic and is deaf into the bargain. But he'd hear nothing from us. My life mate is taciturnity incarnate. I misinterpret significant silence for sullen sulks.

Surely it's not that Capote crack of mine buried now beneath hours of self-induced lockjaw. I let sleeping dogs lie all the way up to 6B, where as I've already noted there's no place to hide. An apartment this size is suitable only for the smaller emotions. Anything bombastic becomes *Ben-Hur* rerun on a Sony. And multiple orgasms (I should imagine) would bring down all the plaster in the bedroom.

But I'm willing to have a civilized nightcap, put on the gloves, and go a few rounds, if that's what's indicated.

I'm alone in the living room, though—just me and the Welsh dresser and the looming loveseat. It's so tomb-quiet in here that I fancy I can hear from all over town the muted pleading from disco queues.

Since Tom isn't in the living room, he's in either the bathroom or the bedroom. Unless he's bought a dog to walk or left me. At the very thought I give one of Hillary's own tense snickers, but keep it quiet. My hand twitches to a pile of reading matter. As research I've been making lists of Yiddish words culled from *New York* magazine. *Chutzpah* I have, but I'm hung up on *bris*.

And it's growing clearer by the minute that I could sit here all night in my lugubrious party frock. There's a nonevent taking places here in 6B, and I don't even have the best seat in the house for it.

I find Tom in the bedroom. He's slumped on the far side of the bed looking away at nothing I can see. Why do I see myself as Jill Clayburgh creeping up on Michael Murphy? He's into his pajama top, but not out of his trousers. Talk about transitional.

Is this boy-man I've been married to since the dawn of time turning enigmatic on me? What's he got up his pajama sleeve?

"Barbara?"

Who else? "Yes?"

A long pause you can hear your heart in. "I don't think I can go on with this. I know I can't."

My mind leaps—too eagerly—to the party and to the career it represents. He picks this up in the air.

"No. Not anything—external."

I'm standing between his back and the light in the hall, casting him in shadow. I notice how dark the room is. Only the idiot Pepsi sign slicing through the blinds from far-off Queens. My hand reaches across the distance for his shoulder but hangs there in the air.

He sighs, or groans. Still he's faced away from me. He rubs his temples. "I want to go back."

Back? My mind thrusts him aside and leaps ahead. I'm already sprinting up Green Bay Road to Walden Woods, leggy and unwinded, with the loveseat strapped to my back. "Back?"

"Back home."

At least we're both headed in the same direction. But I sense there's more to this. I try to form his thoughts into safe shapes. "If you want to quit the job, it's fine with me. I'll get

something. I don't mind going back to work. Maybe not
Leisure Sportswear, but—"

He's shaking his head and I'm trying to read his neck. It's
an obscure blow to my pride that I can't follow his train of
thought. All these years I've been so sure I could, if and
when the need arose. And it's rising like the moon right now.

"No. My old job's still open," he's saying, barely audible.
"They'll give it to me. I'm not the first one who's backed off
from New York."

I wait, vaguely petrified. "Well, then, let's do it. I can
make the big sacrifice. I never got the credit card from Altman's anyway."

Is he angry at one of us? He seems to be working the knots
out of his shoulders. Or writhing.

"I . . ." (What, man, what?) "I'm going back on my own.
I want a divorce."

It's true what you hear about knees. Mine buckle against
the bed. He's not kidding around. He rarely does. I'm the
resident quipster in this . . . family.

"I see," I say from the bottom of a well.

"If we hadn't come to New York," he's saying, "it might
have been different. Maybe I'd have ridden it out. I don't
know. But here . . . I find I can't do without her."

Her.

My mind leaps again and lands spreadeagle in the typing
pool of either Title and Trust or Casualty and Life. Just
which faceless pair of bouncing boobs and steaming ovaries
has played hob with my husband's midlife crisis? I haven't
even the satisfaction of putting a name to this overripe nym-
phet fresh from some remedial stenography college. The
very thought of college conjures up Isabelle Van Donder
parting her lush knees beneath dormitory shrubbery. The
years since are wiped out, and so am I.

"There's someone else," I say. I'm not retarded. I'm only verifying—or playing for time now that it's run out. "Somebody younger than me."

"No, she isn't."

Why this is the final blow, I can't imagine.

"Someone I know."

"You know her slightly."

Something is rising in my throat: either hysteria, sobs, or dinner. "Well, that leaves out Libby." It was hysteria.

"It's Marlene Millsap."

I pitch forward on the bed.

And still I'm light-years from the far side where Tom's still facing away from me into the dark. Marlene Millsap. I haven't thought of her since I lost her list of suburban addresses. Marlene Millsap. Hails from Berwyn, though that only slipped out once. A minor skin condition. Married, one would have thought, to Hube, who's in machinery for earth moving.

And Marlene makes the earth move for Tom? Marlene Millsap? My God, this is a lateral move. He isn't even trading up.

And when? And where? How often? And where was I all that time? The phrase *fool's paradise* rings out like organ music with Ethel Smith at the keyboard. My hindsight is usually 20/20, but I'm drawing blanks all over the bedroom, which at least keeps me quiet. I am inclined at lesser moments than this one to fill up voids of any kind with noise of any sort.

At the door (where am I going, for God's sake?) I say, "I won't beg. I don't know how."

"No. Don't."

He turns around now, and in the dimness I see his face washed clean of the years. Oh, yes, that can happen with men. I hate them all. Every one of them. Except this one. And still he looks exactly the way he did when we were camping out in that art deco apartment by the El in South Evanston and we both still wore penny loafers.

And still I'm at the door, refusing to cling to it. I've got a history with this guy. Has Mr. Amnesia blocked that? What about the time he had hepatitis, and I spoon-fed the Yellow Peril for three solid months. *And* schlepped all those bedpans heaped with pathologically silvery turds? What about that recessional corporate shakeup in '74 and the attendant bout of impotence? What about . . . a lot of times. In and out of bed. In and out of the mood. In and out of love.

"Do you happen to remember the time on that business convention, the one in Los Angeles when we stayed at the Beverly Hills Hotel and everybody around the pool looked like Francis Ford Coppola?"

Tom's willing to humor me. He listens.

"And I went down early to the Polo Lounge for breakfast, and bacon and eggs cost nine dollars. Outside there was that terrace with garden furniture, but nobody was eating out there. And it looked like fur wraps and stoles were draped all over the chair seats and just left there even though it'd rained in the night.

"It was incredibly *Day of the Locust*, and when you came down you thought so too. And then the waiter said they were cats—abandoned house cats gone wild that crept down out of the hills every night to sleep on the furniture and . . . beg at the kitchen door. And sure enough, some of them got up and stretched themselves and wandered off. Don't ask me why I just remembered that. I did, that's all. It just flashed before my eyes—I suppose the rest of my life will too in time. It was just something we did, or saw, or something. It was just . . ."

He waits, doing honor to this blatant non sequitur that streaks shrilly into the night sky and fizzles.

And then he says, "What will you—"

"I don't know what I'll do. How in the hell am I supposed to know? Have I been drawing up contingency plans against the night my husband comes home from eating garbage at the tackiest dinner party in the slummiest town in the muggiest night of modern times and tells me in a monotone that he's trading me in for one of the frumpier hausfraus on the Northshore? I tell you frankly, you've got me stumped. I don't know what I'll do. My plans are in a somewhat earlier stage than yours."

I'm out in the hall, wracking my brain for an epithet to throw over my shoulder at him, but all I can come up with is *faithless shit*, which doesn't even scan.

"You know, Barbara," he says from his dim lair behind me, "we—"

Oh, no, you don't. I whirl back and grab dark air with both hands. "If you're going to say we had some good years, and we ought to be glad of that, you can save your breath, you—"

"I wasn't. I was going to say we made it too easy for each other. We never really tried hard enough."

Who does? "Who does?"

"I don't know," he says to the floor. "Maybe nobody. But you and I, we're just . . . a habit with each other."

"Nothing you can't break, I notice."

"You don't see it, do you," and his voice is like a dull ache. "I look ahead and all I see is—pages dropping off a calendar. I want to start over, in ways we can't."

I'm still not quite believing any of this. "You want a lot for yourself, don't you?"

"I don't know. Maybe . . . it'd be right for you too."

"Oh, spare me that. You're leaving me for my own good? Even if I believed it, you wouldn't."

He's stirring now, edging away, symbolically. "Let's not make this harder than it is. Let's make it . . . civilized."

"Civilized?" My voice is raised now, let the world hear. "It seems to me that's where we went wrong all along. We've been civilized as all get-out, and look where it's led—you going off with the first pathetic old twat who'll talk to you at a party."

"Barbara—"

"You take *civilized* and shove it, buddy," barks this wild woman I've become. "You get your skinny ass out of my life, and you keep it out. Are you listening to me? I want you out of here. I care no more about what happens to you than you care what happens to me. So you just get the hell out of my life, and you keep running till you can't see any more pages falling off calendars or whatever convenient fantasy you dream up next. If you're worrying about growing old, forget it. You never grew up.

"And listen well, I'm going to tell you one more thing, and I want you to take it to heart. When you walk out that door, I don't want to hear *from* you, and I don't want to hear *about* you. When you walk out that door—don't even look back."

He didn't.

CHAPTER 10

THE new man in my life wears a J.C. Penney Windbreaker and Hush Puppies—an ex-con, in fact. I've left the world of corporate resumes for records of another sort. His grin is lopsided and his waist thick. But he sags sensuously, and he's still quick with his fists. Good head of hair on him too.

For half my late marriage, I've lusted for him on the side. Now I'm at leisure to pant for him without impediment. We drive endlessly through stoplights in his old fishtailing Firebird, pursuing and being pursued by the unrighteous.

Reaching out to chuck one of his chins, my hand splays against the picture tube. I've had discreet hots for James Garner ever since *The Americanization of Emily,* and I'm all his now.

The single advantage of New York life is that *The Rockford Files* reruns three nights a week. I am in every sense up for it. And when the occasional special in the public interest interrupts my programming—some hot flash or other about nuclear meltdown or another nation gone People's Republic, I jerk the plug from the wall, telescope the rabbit ears savagely, or switch to Channel 13 and seethe through another documentary on the snail darter.

Increasingly a creature of the night, I'm programmed like the woman directly across the courtyard-airshaft whose apartment is the mirror image of ours. Mine.

She's another Rockford freak, and a solitary. Our Sonys simulcast blue flickers across a matched set of ceilings. And she's in a more advanced state of decay than I, unless I'm glancing up during commercials at my own reflection. And when Garner rolls shirtless from his single bed, her knees part perceptibly beneath pink chenille. She noshes religiously from a sack of Doritos and pokes wisps of whey-colored hair back into a fraying chignon. I consider sending semaphore signals from my sill, but hers, I think, is the misery that does not love company.

Unfortunately Rockford occupies only three hours out of the week. One must make shift to fill the rest. Being dumped gives you every symptom of encephalitis except double vision. But after the first stage of sudden singledom, I stop trying to sleep days. My dreams are grotesque. For one thing—and here comes another imponderable:

I'm always smoking in them. I who never smoked in my life, not even during rush week. The dreams are absolute production numbers in which the garbage-clotted New York streets are also an enormous, pulsating alimentary canal, equally junk-filled, and probably mine, though one distended intestine is wound around my neck. Drop that film loop on Dr. Joyce Brothers and watch her go brunette with shock.

So I tend to leap out of bed in the mornings, moving fast from one nightmare to another. And I've replayed the Tom-tells-Barbara-he's-splitting scene all I'm going to. True, I've embroidered on later versions, adding flung crockery and extra epithets. But its basic structure is too tersely undramatic to play well in a city where any ordinary family reunion degenerates into louder psychodrama. Anyway, our show seems to have closed out of town.

There's probably a hot line for women in my situation, but I've always shied from any organization that adds *Collective* to its name. So, mistaking early shock for clarity, I turn with pathetic confidence to homemade solutions.

Long walks play me false. You need somebody to come home to after running a gauntlet that grim. When I was a New Yorker less alone, I could just manage quick glimpses of the women who live from shopping bags in the shadow of Grand Central, could note their suppurating legs, the raw meat of their mad faces left out in all weathers.

Now, I can manage to get all the way to the bank without going anywhere near their social center at 42nd and Lex.

I select a teller who looks as if she hasn't recently been held at gunpoint and ascertain that the joint checking account hasn't been closed out by orders from Illinois. And so I haven't yet been rendered a nonperson by a computer named Marlene Millsap. If she is Millsap still.

This raises other fundamental questions at the standup desk of Manufacturers Hanover. Conundrums of marital status. Could I be divorced and not know it? Do people still go to Reno? Or step over the border at Juarez? At this very minute could Tom be charging me with mental cruelty or citing my cooking in some foreign clime? And when I told him I never wanted to hear from him again, was I really thinking ahead?

Drawing an experimentally exorbitant check against our

former marriage, I find it bounceless and seem not to want to know more.

"Have a nice day," the teller tells me.

One nice day I'll go to the bank and find the cupboard bare. I scan Help Wanted in the *Times*. Since I'm having my own emotional recession, I'm not intimidated by a drying job market. Anything that smacks of retail trade—the barest hint of Leisure Sportswear—is out. I'm not sure I'd turn back the clock if I could; I'm only sure I can't.

And with the luck of beginners and fools, I discover quite a different kind of job, for a day—hired by a bus tour company on the strength of a midwestern accent that allows me to pronounce the middle *d*s and *t*s of any word I care to speak.

To add substance to this style, I've done extensive research on the city: the perimeters of SoHo, the several statistics of the World Trade Center, and what Viollet-le-Duc had to do with the Statue of Liberty.

On my only day of employment in the tourist industry, I report to the bus girded with an amusing anecdote about Trinity Church burial ground, only to find behind the bus driver, who's smoking a cupped joint and beginning to roll before the rest of us, a full payload of West German tourists.

They're Cyclopsean with Leicas and all of a single, intermediate sex, though some wear stubby Cuban-heeled gray snakeskin pumps, planted in the aisle. My name tag gives greetings in seven languages. I take a shot at "*Willkommen, meine Damen und Herren.*"

"Good day," says one vast Valkyrie in chill reply. She is blank of mien and hairy of armpit, in a sleeveless blouse, or perhaps two sewn together. She's also spokesperson for the group, whom I suspect darkly of being English speakers all and former death camp attendants on holiday. I've boned up especially on Greenwich Village and can do an entire shtik on TriBeCa, but the driver hands me the itinerary, and it must be a typo because it's for the South Bronx.

"Surely not," I mutter to myself. The Valkyrie riding shotgun picks up on that. "You do not show us this, you show us that, we are to look yes here, no there? This is perhaps East Berlin?"

The Bitch of Buchenwald flares a knowing nostril at her compatriots, and they nod knowingly back.

We do the South Bronx. Narration is superfluous, for my charges spend the trip with enormous knees planted on the seats, shooting roll after roll of film across leveled landscapes, bloodstained sidewalks, half-torched tenements all too obviously still occupied. A stripped pimpmobile on its axles is good for a roll apiece right down the aisle.

Eons later we're at last tooling back across the Third Avenue Bridge. The Master Race settle back in their seats, well satisfied. "Ah," says the Valkyrie, summing up, "you do to yourselves what you haf done to us."

I resign, foreseeing the eventuality of a busload of Japanese ordering me to Three Mile Island.

But feeling vague stirrings of spunk for want of being able to feel anything else, I look for another job. Will anyone want a serious look at my college record with its three minors and no major?

Not at a temporary office-help agency unpromisingly called Gals Friday. Nor should they, paying so close to minimum. Any organization thus named could of course deal in all sorts of temporary services that land you in a lineup. But this place has the sober aura of a bankrupt business college. I'm given a typing test on which I receive the moral equivalent of a C−.

The woman in charge, whose idea of a joke is to impersonate Edith Bunker down to the washdress, sends me, without a lot of encouragement, to my first assignment.

I set off with the address, trying to determine where Park Avenue ends and Park Avenue South begins and catch glimpses of myself in passing plate glass. I've dressed as a temp: nondescript sweater and uncoordinated skirt. Flats. Nails filed to typing length. My makeup is minimal.

It occurs to me that I'm abasing myself before the head of some typing pool has her first chance to. This is, I see it now, the Lent of my life. And I may have said so aloud, because oncoming pedestrians move sharply out of my path.

Yes. I'm almost sure of it as I rise in the elevator to the offices of something called The Hergesheimer Group. I'm punishing myself. Have I not just force-marched myself down Park Avenue South, head shaved and spit-spattered, for having collaborated (unsuccessfully) with the enemy—men?

I am a penitential temp. But am I only temporarily penitential? Or will this go on and on in a downward spiral. Failing inevitably in the typing pool amid cleft palates from Queens, will I next be scrubbing the floors beneath their Papagallos?

The elevator opens onto The Hergesheimer Group. I expect some female straw boss wielding a time card and a whip. Instead, a little old man is waiting with clasped hands, obviously for me. White wisps of hair across a pink dome. Antique specs. A darling little old alpaca suit with a rosebud in the buttonhole. He looks like Edmund Gwenn. And his bottom-pinching days are behind him and not me.

He's ever so glad to see me too. Because the receptionist (Dear old Rosemarie) who's been with the firm from the first is out getting a pin in her hip. While remaining faithful to her, the old gent manages to imply that, temp though I be, I might get tenure here. He twinkles at me, and I'm bowed into Rosemarie's front-office swivel chair.

After he shows me ten things I still don't understand about the phone system, he bows himself out. Only at the door, in an agony of modesty, does he reveal himself as Mr. Hergesheimer.

The day lengthens eerily, and I sit through it in solitary grandeur in the airless, well-appointed room. No one calls and no one arrives. I try to remember what receptionists do, but my nails are already down to the quick and I've left all my cosmetics at home. Ready to take the veil, I'm instead a bird in a gilded cage. Mr. Hergesheimer takes an early lunch and brings back a bouquet of asters for my desk. Why is it that the last of the real gentlemen are pushing eighty?

The only afternoon phone call is obscene. I have been dialed at random and asked to fondle my own breasts, somehow audibly, into the receiver.

At three, Mr. Hergesheimer brings *me* coffee and turns ashen when he realizes I didn't go out for lunch. I'm sent home immediately.

I last a week, becoming a virtual Rosemarie. He has three calls, two about a poker party and one from the United Jewish Appeal. I insist on making him coffee, bearing it to his office, and wake him from a light slumber to drink it.

On Friday his sons arrive: Maurie and Teddy. I've heard about them all week—the attorney and the ad man. They spring conspiratorially from the elevator in Paul Stuart suits and Italian shoes.

This is my first chance to announce anybody, but they breeze past me. "How's it going, Rosemarie?" says one of them as they disappear into Dad's office.

They're in there a long time. Mr. Hergesheimer buzzes and asks me to hold all calls. I play along. It's probably evening by the time the three of them emerge. I seem to know what's coming.

I've been in business, but has Mr. Hergesheimer? Has he only been holding on here, superannuated, in a front for his own valiant dotage? Have his sleek, brutish sons come to force his retirement?

Yes.

The three are crossing the reception room now. One son carries a very small file drawer; the other, an early adding machine with a crank. Mr. Hergesheimer, suspended between them, is shrunken. His boys have blown his cover, there's the horror of Miami Beach in his watering eyes.

"Fifty-four years in the same location," he says quietly. Still some dignity left. "And two big shots put through college who never wanted for a thing."

"Now, Dad," they say. "Now, Dad."

They give him the bum's rush right past me. "And what about Miss Renfrew?" he wants to know, stamping a small, shiny shoe.

I have taken Miss Renfrew as my professional name.

The sons stare in surprise at my un-Rosemarieness. But I am revealed as a temp and dismissed.

I wait until they leave. There's nothing to lock up—or steal. I sit there in the gloom, and a single tear for Mr. Hergesheimer falls on my blotter.

I'm not tough enough for temp work. I counted on light typing, not *Death of a Salesman*. I retire and return to the licking of my own wounds. Miss Renfrew, crackerjack receptionist, becomes old broken Bubbles again.

Like many of the chronically afflicted, I misread the symptoms of my disease for stages in its recovery. Confidently, almost, I look for convalescence in Greenacre Park, that storefront-size oasis on 51st Street, and sit—not quite on the street yet—through long, unmanageable mornings under a paling sun.

Near the waterfall that drowns the traffic sounds, I sit drinking coffee from a paper cup and dividing a Danish with deliberation.

Refusing to rerun *Scenes from a Marriage*, I mean to find a little peace here in the park. And when my mind threatens to start missing that skunk, Tom Renfrew, I can usually turn it off. But still I flash back.

One ominous morning I'm nearly jolted off my park bench by a sudden, unbidden vignette from the past. It involves, of all people, Libby Smallwood.

I'm wrenched back to her dining room table on some long-ago day, staring into an epergne tight with her massed straw-flowers. It's that time she'd sat me down to speak circumlocutions about a certain straying husband. I flinch at the memory, and coffee leaps out of the paper cup. Because, oh, dear God, Libby'd been trying to tell me about *my* husband, not hers.

No. This is one delayed epiphany I can't cope with. I must banish it from my brain, but blush-red leaves are straying down from the park trees, reminding me insistently of Libby's permanent arrangements, while around me the gardeners are planting an autumnal display. They surround my square of brickwork with chrysanthemums. I regard the effect gravely.

There's always just time to make a lunch date with myself and to stand in the heavily symbolic Singles Only line at some department store's luncheonette.

The midday streets are thronged with couples courting on their lunch hour, scuffing heedless through trash, arms and eyes fatally entwined. I stifle shrieks of warning at them. The well-known breaking point and I are on a collision course, and I half know it.

But this moment of truth is forestalled. I return from a self-pitying lunch at Bergdorf's bleak counter to find a stampless envelope under 6B's door. I read all communiqués from the outside world with avidity and am responding well to being addressed as Occupant.

This envelope bears the imprint of the co-op board. Sensing fresh rejection, I wonder if I still own my apartment. Am I about to face eviction at the hands of a couple of long-in-the-tooth lovebirds starting over in Walden Woods? I reduce the envelope to rubble on the way to the letter.

Fortunately, it's mimeographed, and if I would just not get so panicky, I could see that it's a form letter for everybody in the building. It informs us more in sorrow than in anger that the extortionate demands of the custodians' union contract proposal cannot be met without threatening the national inflation rate. The result is a strike of our staff. For the duration of this outrage, we're urged to rally round, keep our garbage to ourselves, and sign up for voluntary duty.

I'm already out at the elevator, slavering to sign on for anything to take me out of myself and 6B. This is how the French Foreign Legion got to be such a big deal. Scanning the options, I skip "Laundry room clean-up," skim "Mail sorting," come to rest on "Doorpersons—2-hour shifts," and lean on the down button.

It's well known that crises galvanize New Yorkers. Our lobby is crawling with raddled crones as desperate as I for novelty. To sign on as doorperson, I have to push senior citizenesses out of the way. I volunteer in every blank space for the foreseeable future.

The real doormen are working their last day and getting a bad snubbing from our side. All this militant counterinsurgency is striking fear in the eyes of the Puerto Rican porters who are giving the lobby doorplates a final polish before they can retreat to their side of the barricades.

The strike is on now. I've turned into a human trash compactor. My daily tin of Campbell's soup is jammed with the detritus of feminine hygiene into a granola box and topped off with hairbrush leavings and yogurt tubs folded into origami. I make special trips to the overflowing trashcan at 49th and First to make my drop.

My first doorperson duty is an evening shift. We work in pairs: one to announce guests on the vintage intercom, the other to spot for rapists swinging from the canopy outside. In theory, this duty is supposed to be mixed doubles. But here in women's prison the males are not thick upon the ground. Either we've outlived our men or they've outdistanced us. Besides, I suspect the men in the building of malingering. I suspect men of a great deal these days as I seek to diffuse localized pain.

It's regarded as mildly unpatriotic to entertain during the strike, putting pressure upon us voluntary doorpeople. Still, planned parties are going forth, and I receive the guests of perfect strangers. Three C gives smart blacktie do's and seems to have seating for eight; 9L runs rendezvous for near-kin of the Manson family; 14P gives gay parties. My neighbors begin to quiver with identity.

My first fellow doorperson is not a success. Heavily hung with the diamonds of many alliances, she seems to have discovered the hairdresser of the late Martha Mitchell. And she rants at length that the doormen are better paid than those of us on fixed incomes.

Even with reading glasses on a chain, she cannot see to dial the intercom. And ever since both her wrists were broken when she was flung down the steps of the Flushing line by a group of unwed mothers on a field trip, her doctor has forbidden her to open doors. I have a busy evening.

My second shift is with Miss Mapes, another gentlewoman of the old school. Though she's the desiccated spinster of British fiction, she speaks in the aggrieved whine of the native New Yorker. On this linguistic evidence, I have confused civility with crankiness before, and indeed Miss Mapes is civil to a fault, in her way. And subtle. She brings her bargello, sign enough that if there's jumping up and door opening to be done, I'm to do it. She compensates by being informative about everybody in the building and reiterates how lucky I am to be in one of the last of the Really Nice Buildings.

"The secret of our success," she says, sweetly stabbing her canvas, "is the smallness of our apartments. We have never attracted the Jews."

Miss Mapes has the us-and-them mentality of New York down pat. She has not a word against anyone in our building. All the remaining men are charming and all the women have borne up wonderfully. When old Mr. Venable shuffles in from a long day on a park bench, smelling like a colostomy bag, she recalls the fine figure he cut before the crash of '29 brought him low.

When a call girl in a purple crew cut and Fiorucci body stocking arrives for 2A, Miss Mapes posits that she's 2A's niece. And when 14P gives his second gay party in as many nights—this one a real bash—Miss Mapes refers to the gathering as a "smoker."

I'm nearly lulled by this sanitized version of reality. On our second shift together, Miss Mapes identifies a strapping young stud who breezes in, door key at the ready, as "Mrs. Elphinstone's grandson," and my tongue is hardly in my cheek at all. I'm rather down on men at the moment but this doesn't extend to boys. I watch the alleged grandson all the way to the elevator. Construction boots, nondesigner jeans, good Harris tweed jacket, collar turned up against a mop of sandy curls.

But Miss Mapes is extolling his Grandmother Elphinstone and expects me to pay attention. Mrs. Elphinstone is the pillar of our community. She has been a great beauty and has given her life to good works.

She ran soup kitchens in the thirties, canteens in the forties, spoke out against McCarthy in the fifties, sold her Dow stock in the sixties and her car in the seventies, withdrew her support for the Olympics in eighty, and has borne up wonderfully since.

It's a great pity that I can't meet her, because she's just gone down to Aiken for the fall foliage. But a few more strokes from Miss Mapes' brush and I realize I have met her already. She's the female flasher in the floor-length mink.

With Miss Mapes I enjoy perfect anonymity. If she's noticed that I once had a husband that I seem to have misplaced, she makes no mention. And how she knows the name of everybody in the building but seems not to have caught mine, I also cannot comprehend. Apparently all the introductions that are ever going to be made have been. I miss the glad hands, the hypocritical salutations, the hearty exchanges of names that are a feature of strangers meeting in the Midwest. I miss America. Have I said that already? Miss Mapes repeats herself too.

And I might have known that she'd be knowledgeable about the former tenant-owner of 6B. Though my quarters aren't haunted, exactly, they reverberate unpleasantly with somebody's vibrations, which aren't to be confused with my almost continual quaking.

Miss Mapes creeps up on the subject by mentioning how the building is "beginning to turn over" as an earlier generation lives out their normal lifespans, and in Mrs. Elphin-

stone's case, then some. I'm thoroughly braced by now to
hear the fate of 6B's earlier occupant, poor Mrs. Weillup. I
long to stop my ears, but there is no stopping Miss Mapes.

Poor Mrs. Weillup lived to a ripe age in 6B, consistently
robbed in her senility by a succession of pack-rat practical
nurses. She was down to her last pistol-grip fruit knife when
she was found dead of natural causes in her bath. I blanch.
Found several days later, she was roughly the shape of the
bathtub. I cower. This is not the first dead body I've ever
heard of found lying around a New York apartment, but
still . . .

"Very sad," Miss Mapes says, busy with bright wools,
"but so lucky for *you*."

By my third shift I'm practically a treasured old family re-
tainer. And it seems I'm to be spared Miss Mapes this time,
but my new partner is tardy. I can wait. I straighten unclaimed mail on the refectory table, pinch brown blooms
from the floral display, dust the armor, get a little chatty
with UPS men, and generally run a tight lobby.

A half an hour late, my colleague comes on duty. I barely
avoid looking at my watch and tapping my foot. I've seen
this one before. It's my fellow Rockford freak, the Doritos
muncher from across the airshaft. I had thought her face
blurred by two windows, but no, she's still a little blurred
and smelling faintly of chili powder and Dewars.

When *I'm* on duty, I wear a trim blazer and no-nonsense
pumps, like a Bunny Mother. But my partner rises to no oc-
casions. She is wearing a gingham duster and the kind of
bedroom slippers you can pack.

"Oh, Christ, what do we have to *do*?" She sinks moaning
onto a porter's stool, throwing one bare leg over the other.
The veins in her calves are beginning to spider.

We neither of us have much to do. This is the eight-to-ten
shift, and our asylum seems to be tucked in for the night.

"You're 6D?" I say, still a little gregarious from my UPS men. She betrays no surprise at this knowledge.

"That's right. And if I was going to be on with that Mapes woman tonight, I wouldn't have stayed. She's 7D, and the bitch bangs on the floor constantly if I have the TV on past nine o'clock. Honestly, this place is a fucking zoo. I hate it. New York sucks, don't you think?"

I goggle, trying to make the transition from Mapes to this. Dirty talker that she is, though, anybody with that attitude toward New York has her standards.

"I can tell you, I'd go back if I could."

"Back where?"

"Anywhere in the whole motherfucking world is where."

There really is something about her I like.

I settle onto a stool opposite, ready to hear her life story, which is quite clearly crying out to be told. She runs a finger down her duster's drooping armhole, snaps a bra strap, and begins running her existence backward through a mental movieola.

Men have brought her to her present state. Three husbands that she names, though there's no point in repeating the names she calls them. And they all wanted but one thing from her, so I assume the last one has been gone some years.

She has children too, though she's retained custody of none of them, one small counterbalancing triumph in her life. The other is that she got 6D out of a divorce settlement. Which is at least something, except that it's in New York and directly under "that repressed dyke with the broom handle." I nearly miss this reference to Miss Mapes popping up in our conversation again.

"When I think how glamorous New York used to sound to me when I was a kid out in the Middle West. Sonofabitch, make you puke."

I've already figured she's from west of here. Sloppy

though her speech is, she can pronounce the *g* in *strength* and *length*.

I confess that I'm from her neck of the woods.

"Yeah, I can see. New, though, aren't you?" She wafts an unmanicured hand generally in my direction. "After a while, why bother?" She's clearly referring to my Bunny Mother grooming. "You get all dolled up, you go to the beauty parlor, and for what? Where's there to *go*?"

I'm damned if I know. "New York isn't quite as—dressy as I'd thought." I try not to look her in the wardrobe.

"*Dressy*?" she spits. "If you're thinking dressy, you're thinking Minneapolis. I just go down to May's and buy what they've got. What the fuck's the difference?" She scoots up her skirt and scratches above her knee. She only shaves partway up. "Remember maple bars?" she says, out of the blue.

Somehow I don't.

"You know, those long pastry things with maple icing on top? Have you tasted the pastries in this town? Everything dry as a goddamn bone and prune-filled."

I do remember maple bars, now that she mentions them.

"God, I could eat a dozen. There was this little place where we used to have them with coffee between classes." There's sudden, dreamy distance in 6D's eyes. "This little greasy-spoon hangout right off campus. Holy shit, was that a long time ago. I had a poly sci class that actually met there." Her eyes go bovine in a matching face. Her knees are parting again, and faint bells are tolling in my inner recesses.

"A little hangout right off campus?" I echo.

Six-D nods, lost in thought. "Dumpy little dive with pennants. Did their own baking."

"The Ruptured Rooster," I say, half sure.

Six D nods, dreamy still. Then jerks upright. "Yeah, as a matter of fact." I have at last gained her full attention. "Say, listen, who the fuck are you anyway?"

"I married Tom Renfrew."

She squints at me, and a hand worries her chignon. "Sigma Nu? Jock? Journalism?"

"Sigma Chi. Jock. Econ."

"Yeah, that's about right. Married him. The hell you did."

"The hell I didn't," I say genially to what was once Isabelle Van Donder.

CHAPTER 11

WITH nowhere to turn, I'm dressing to go out anyway, and with some care, though it's only to deposit my garbage, wrapped today in silver paper, the stretch bow by Lord & Taylor.

The strike's over, and so we scabs are jobless. Isabelle has returned to 6D. Neither of us was eager to form an alumnae club. I suspect her of despair and dare not know her better.

Strike or no strike, I'm still taking my garbage for walks. One needs a destination, if only a wire basket. Aimlessness is where those Grand Central women went astray. And I don't carry my gift-wrapped garbage in a shopping bag either; I know the early signs.

Miss Mapes is in the lobby as I glide purposefully through. She's explaining to Pedro the porter that in Red

China he wouldn't have been allowed to strike at all and that in Afghanistan he'd be dead by now. Nodding, Pedro grins too fast to have comprehended, so she starts again with him. My hand closes over the doorman's fist on the knob. His small, reproachful smile is to remind me that the strike's over, and he bows me out.

Today my route takes me past Turtle Bay Gardens, the heart of Katharine Hepburn country. I scan this facade of town houses that anywhere but Newark or here would either have been cleaned up or razed. And I wonder if Katharine herself, hand stroking bound neck, might be glancing down from a drawing room this minute, remarking my passage.

Hers is the only full block around where the basement apartments are not mostly psychiatrists' offices. In these parts, the head doctors are outnumbered only by the leg waxers.

I've never been to a psychiatrist, mainly because I've never thought I could help him. But I'm reasonably sure Miss Hepburn would have a ready solution for my case. There's a woman who's known exactly how to fill a lifetime with pleasure, profit, and the occasional man. Also, whatever the role, she's always gotten away with playing herself. On the other hand, her patience might run thin with me, who at the first trouble turns into a zombie organizing her day around the disposal of household trash. I slink out of her range in case I'm in it.

And return to 6B where the TV tray is already laid for luncheon for one. In happier days, my best diet plan was the consumption of my own cooking. But now I balance little bijou meals and line up the flatware and fold a linen napkin into a cunning cornet. I am gradually becoming an autoerotic Irma S. Rombauer.

Playing waitress and lady by turns, I shake out the napkin and slip into my place just as it settles on my knees. A single

aster nods in a jelly glass above a bowl of bright gazpacho. I
consider table talk but keep it inaudible, like humming,
which even the sane do solo. And beg my pardon to reach
into the kitchenette for a miniature omelet, parsley-
bedecked.

We round off lunch with a dollop of Häagen-Dazs topped
with a cherry. I make it last. And yet, dammit all anyhow,
I'm still eight hours from Rockford.

Afternoon finds me in the middle of the living room floor
in that cozy gulley between the loveseat and the Welsh
dresser. I'm still pertly dressed in my going-out gear, right
down to autumn taupe pantyhose and footgear innocent of
hardware. The only jarring note in this scene is that I'm
lying face down and screaming uncontrollably into the rug.

Thunder rumbles from my pounding fists and the percus-
sion of well-shod toes. The kickpleat at the back of my knees
is no doubt flapping like a spinnaker in a typhoon.

I've fallen apart in the dead center of the living room and
my life. And in the midst of twelve million sullen strangers.
I'm screaming without restraint in rage and fear, loosing
demons left and right. The rug darkens with tears in a sodden sunburst around my puffing face. I inhale great shuddering gasps of nylon pile. I go on quite a while.

After a time, I'm out of my head, which seems the way to
go. The room's grown dim, and I may have howled my way
to twilight.

But no. The shadow is from another source. My pounding
fist makes contact with noncarpet. I'm faintly aware that I'm
pounding leather: the toe of a construction boot. This stops
me almost at once.

I loll on the other arm, squint through bottomless blur-
riness to see the yellow boot planted not six inches from my
cheekbone. The novelty of this surreal touch almost brings

me around, though my sobs are fetching up with their own momentum.

Still, I follow upward from the boot to a jeaned leg. And where there's one, there are almost always two. Yes, somewhere in my peripheral vision another booted foot is planted.

I roll over onto my back, beginning to feel at a tremendous social disadvantage. Six feet above, I can just make out a face looking down. Crazed still, I grab my own wrist and strain to see what time it is. In better moments than this, I have trouble reading a wristwatch, so why am I trying to now? Possibly some damaged brain cell is frantically signaling that I must have invited a group in for cocktails and that I've been surprised by an early arrival.

I'm one of the lesser-known hostesses in America and have met no one in New York I'd care to have an entire drink with. Still, the cocktail party idea is dying hard because the alternative is that I have an intruder on my hands who may soon be all over me. And this isn't the building superintendent either, because he doesn't make housecalls.

I grunt softly at what may be the Turtle Bay Strangler, the Beast of Beekman, the Pervert from Over on Park, or even Jack Nicholson wielding an axe. Both my ears are brimming with left-over tears. I stay sprawled.

"Mrs. Renfrew?"

Oh, Lord, they won't leave you alone in this town.

"Ms.," I mumble. "Mzzzz."

"Whatever." There's a boyish tone in even these first syllables, and the cautious concern of a neophyte paramedic.

I struggle up on elbows, mine, and notice a hand, his, emerging from a turned-back lumberjacket cuff and reaching down my way. It's heading for neither my throat nor my crotch so I need only decide whether or not to shake it.

"Are you sick or something?" The hand has sought one of mine and is helping me up.

"Something," I mutter, half up, then down on one Play-Doh knee, then all the way up. I refuse to stagger, though drunkenness would be such an easy explanation. My hair seems to be standing out in a honky Afro, and I've made some turns my pantyhose have not.

It's hard to know who owes whom the first explanation. I'm standing level with his collarbone. Unready for eye contact, I look down. In one hand he's holding a bunch of door keys, mine undoubtedly among them. And since the key ring doesn't attach to his belt loop, he's apparently neither the handyman nor a homosexual.

We begin to speak simultaneously, though what I was about to say is anybody's guess. We then take a step back from each other as in one of the stiffer English country dances, and I dare meet his gaze. There's something familiar about this kid, but I can't place him.

He's starting on his explanation first, which should give me time to work up something face-saving for my turn. I chance a look at his extremely pleasant but bemused face and then I concentrate on his upper torso, which is well developed under the lumberjacket and a T-shirt in athletic department gray. His shoulders are roughly the width of Shubert Alley.

It seems he occupies 5B, directly, as luck would have it, beneath 6B. He came home, by his reckoning at three thirty, to hear fists hammering his ceiling and wracking sobs emanating from his overhead light fixture. "You were still at it at four o'clock," he adds, with a touch of the police blotter in his tone.

I'm so patently guilty of this charge that I can only hang my head. My gaze falls again on the key ring.

"You have a full set?" I inquire, trusting he realizes I mean the keys.

He nods. "Actually, they're my grandmother's—Mrs. El-

phinstone's." This is meant to be explanation enough. And I
begin to place him. This is not, after all, Mr. Goodbar. This
is the kid said to be the furry flasher's grandson.

"You're Mrs. Elphinstone's grandson—really."

"Really."

I wipe my nose on my sleeve. It's too late to worry over
first impressions. "And let me guess. Grandmother Elphinstone has a key for every apartment in the building."

"And all the fire doors."

"And she probably has a wonderfully airtight reason too."

He has the grace to look abashed, though people challeng-
ing his grandmother's authority are not thick on the ground,
or the carpet, around here.

"Well, you know," he says, scratching high up on his
flaxen curls, "she figures there are so many elderly people in
the building, she ought to be able to check on them once in a
while. In fact, she was the one who found—"

"Poor Mrs. Weillup."

"Right."

"Figures."

He's rubbing his square chin with a square hand. As a
rule, I'm not awed by urban lumberjacks, but this one is almost authentic. There's what looks like real soil under his
fingernails. He notices my noticing and plants both hands in
his back pockets.

My game plan for the next move crystallizes. I'll divert his
attention from all that embarrassing horizontal screaming and
floor pounding. I'll chat him all the way to the door on
unrelated topics and get rid of him. Get the key back too.

"You're going to find this hard to believe," I say, jockeying
to line him up with the foyer, "but ever since another of this
building's intrusive busybodies told me graphically the shape
and shade of Mrs. Weillup when they fished her out of my
bathtub with a net, I haven't been able to set foot in it

myself. I can't even make myself take a shower. I've been bathing in the sink."

That's true, and I'm almost tapping the point home on his chest, and he's almost walking backward. "Moreover, I never go near the tub without thinking I can smell putrifying flesh."

He clears his throat, pulls a calming hand from a hip pocket. "No, listen, Mrs. Renfrew, don't sweat that. We get that smell all over the building. It isn't Mrs. Weillup."

There is utter silence while I search his face for smirks. Nothing. I crumple. Just when I had him passing backwards into the foyer too. "Oh, for Chrissakes," I hear me saying, "sit down and have a drink.

"You're old enough to drink, aren't you?"

He's looking down at me from a great height, and I think maybe I've possibly said something just a little insensitive. He wears glasses—serviceable round rims. His eyes—cornflower, graying in the dusk of the room—are a little wounded. "I'm twenty-three years old, lady. Give me a break."

For two cents I would.

CHAPTER 12

ERRIER and water?" I offer siren-
like from the sink, testing him. But
this gilded youth was not born
yesterday, quite. He takes Scotch and nurses it unostenta-
tiously on the loveseat, from where his knees jut far out into
the room. He's the healthiest-looking human being I've ever
seen outside California.

We're starting over. I settle into the miniature bergère, in
one more situation where I feel the need to establish my
sanity before a skeptical world. We do not establish that, but
we do determine that his name is Ed—Kimbell, not Elphinstone. That my name is Barbara—not Mrs., not Ms., not
lady; not Barbie or Bubbles.

He parks his glass between his knees, dries a vast hand on
his lumberjacket, and extends it. This is the same mitt that

recently picked the Madwoman of Chaillot off the floor. We shake.

We also establish that he's occupying his grandmother's apartment in her absence.

"While she's down in Aiken for the foliage," I contribute. In the local manner, he betrays no surprise at my knowing this. I might have read it in the Court Circular.

He's never lived with his grandmother; nobody has, "not even Grandfather." And he hopes to have his own place before the last leaf falls on Aiken.

He's four months out of a master's degree in landscape architecture and into a job with a reputable firm. They've got him on cost estimates and speculative designs for high-rise lobbies and penthouse garden plantings. He's been donating his off-hours to the plantings in our building's roof garden. All that topsoil under his nails is honestly come by. A landscape architect in New York? I have unearthed a gardener in a garbage dump.

I seem to be interviewing him talk-show style. My tone turns rather Jessica Savitch. And he's less monosyllabic than one expects from a generation who learned their phonemes one at a time from Big Bird and can remember no historical figure before Squeaky Fromm. True, he says *really* when he means *yes*, and *for sure* when he means *certainly*. But he's steering clear of *hopefully* and hasn't said *laid back* though he certainly is.

However, I'm beginning to sound less like Jessica and more like Barbara Walters at her most drearily staccato, with even the little gasp between the words to take up the slack. All I lack is the lisp, and as I begin to think he's humoring me, I begin to taper off. That gives him the chance to ask if I'd like to look at his roof garden handiwork.

I try desperately not to rocket out of the chair. I'll gladly look at his *al fresco* etchings. I'll go anywhere to get free of

6B. Have I not already organized whole afternoons around watching people trail their Shih Tzus with pooper scoopers? Right now I'm especially anxious to quit this room because there's still a halo of damp on the carpet at our feet, where so recently my head has leaked. I'll follow him and his floral offerings anywhere. You *can* lead a horticulture. I rise in silence, leaving all this prudently unsaid.

It's tawdry twilight in the streets below, but up on the roof garden level, the sun's still setting. And showing off in a baroque display of pink and gold. White fire strikes off the Citicorp's wedge top. The Chrysler Building needles a deepening sky in purest silver. The great steaming dung heap of Manhattan gives way to country gardens hanging like Babylon from its upper elevations. Whole deciduous trees are beginning to celebrate select autumns in the dooryards of Sutton Place penthouses.

I've been up on this roof before of course. On muggy midsummer nights with a husband I used to have. We'd carry our rationed ice cubes up in glasses that sweated circles on the sooty tiles. I see they've put the lawn chairs away. I spot no clues to my former existence up here, which is another point in its favor. Of course the place was a cramped postage stamp to me then. Now, twenty uninterrupted square feet compare favorably with the Fertile Crescent.

Ed gives me the tour of his planters—redwood that he's knocked together to border the parapets and make the most of the space. He's banked and clumped the marigolds and fashioned a windbreak against the elevator housing for the Michaelmas daisies, to keep them unnipped into October. He seems bent on creating Versailles in gutters and leaders. He's squatting on his heels now, running gardener's hands in under the heads of mums, turning up their bright football faces for me to admire. Green-thumbing them with square, practiced hands.

There's something about that vast plaid back bowed to its life's work, something young and elemental and unjaded, that's making me perilously emotional again. He's bringing either the mother or the maniac out in me, but what can I do? In my present state I'm moved by lesser stuff: commercials wherein both newlyweds learn perfect coffee from Mrs. Olsen, the contestant who gets three in a row on *Hollywood Squares*. And right now the lump in my throat is a case for Roto-Rooter.

I turn from Ed's brief treatise on the genus *Gentiana* and plant my elbows on a parapet. As I'm on the edge again, I must not be too literal in my thinking up here. I stare down the canyons to the ends where the Hudson is still half on fire.

Ed has gauged my attention span for botany and is filling a watering can from a tap. I keep my back to him and admire the view swimming before me. He must not see me like this again.

I'm crying quietly at the skyline. Directly below, a gargoyle's pitted cheeks are running real tears. I'm trying to keep my shoulders squared and my head erect. If there must be tears, at least let us avoid the flailing extremities. I could even cry myself out here, rigid as an extra griffin, and dry up before I'm discovered again.

But, no. On and on I go, weeping at attention.

He's stepped up behind me, and his hands, very untentative, are cupping my shoulders. "You've got a lot to let out, haven't you?" he says quietly, right into my ear.

"Really," I manage.

"For sure," he says.

The next thing I remember with any certainty is the interior of a place called the Spring Street Tavern in SoHo, a filthy, fashionable warehouse district. The decor is utilitar-

ian, and except for a covey of middle-aged vultures on bar-
stools scanning the room through contact lenses, I appear to
be the token adult in the place.

And what I'm doing here is having a schooner of Heinekens and a light supper with neighborly Ed. He's either
given to acts of charity or has taken me out to liquor me up
so that I'll go quietly to sleep tonight and not commit tattoos
on his ceiling.

This must be a singles bar, but I've walked past Maxwell's
Plum and it doesn't have that feel. For one thing, the lighting
in this place is pitiless. And no one seems frantic but me.
The conversations are subdued hums; the whole ambiance is
stark and straight. True, some of the tykes at the next table
are smoking things down to their knuckles in a manner that
arouses speculation. But they also seem to be discussing
grain futures. As usual, I'm disoriented. I mention to Ed that
this spa seems a distant variant upon Maxwell's Plum.

The name rings a faint bell with him. "The place up on
Second Avenue? I think my aunt used to go there."

I'm sitting with my purse on my knees; everybody else's
hangs from a strap. Of course I mean to pay for our supper,
but I must manage it so that it doesn't seem I'm buying him
by the dance. Oh, Lord, give me guidance. Here come the
hamburgers, sunk beneath cartwheels of onion. I pitch into
this far cry from my dollhouse food.

While making rather a show of mastication, I find I can't
continue this charade without explaining. I make a game
beginning.

"You must have thought, this afternoon, that I was
being—attacked . . . something like that."

"Not necessarily," he says, connecting the wet rings on the
table with a random finger. "I just figured you were a little
ticked. About, you know, Mr. Renfrew taking off."

Hamburger lurches in my throat, crying out for the Heimlich Maneuver. I must have emitted a startled sound because the foursome at the next table turns heads in our direction.

Searching for a level tone, I say, "You know, Ed, I tell you frankly, I find New York a very difficult town to get along in—the combination of intense loneliness coupled with the astonishing invasion of privacy. It really is the worst of all possible worlds. Really."

While he absorbs this slander upon his city, I rethink my position. Is there a hint of the ingrate in my manner? After all, he could have let me lie there on my living room floor until I ran down. Or even dialed 911 on me. Instead of having a matey hamburger with this comely stripling, I could be hanging from my wrists behind a door at Bellevue this minute, trying even more desperately to explain.

Ed rubs his chin again. Is that peach fuzz or does he shave? "You're from the Middle West, right?"

I narrow swollen eyes at him. "I don't recall having said so."

"Didn't have to," he replies, grinning. And it's a grin not unlike Rockford's. "I had a roommate at college from Mankato, Minnesota. She talked funny too."

I fall back in my chair at this final outrage but let it pass in the interest of hearing more. Though I murmur to the effect that I've never been in Mankato in my life.

"Where are you from?" he asks.

"Chicago."

"Bullshit. Suburbia sticks out all over you."

I bridle again. But then I catch a glimpse of a girl at the next table who's also in Ed's sight line. She has permanent curvature of the spine and dowager's hump at nineteen. She's wearing four unlaundered layers of mosquito netting, and the ankle of one leg is planted on the knee of the other. One of her ankle straps is broken and uncurling from a shapeless leg. A Hunter College handbook peeps from an unraveling raffia totebag. And she's picking her nose.

With a significant look at her and a touch of pride, I plead guilty to the suburban charge.

"I grew up in Scarsdale," he says. "My mom still lives there." We determine that I hail from Walden Woods.

"A little place?"

"Select."

"What's the population?"

Why men always want to know the population of places is one more sex-linked trait that baffles and annoys me. "I have no idea. We just take the Indian Hill Country Club membership directory and divide by four."

Ed scrunches down in his chair, toys with the beer mug handle. One of his denimed knees rises before me, and I find myself staring straight into his crotch. I stop almost at once.

"For the sake of argument," he's saying, "let's say Walden Woods has a hundred and fifty households. That near enough?"

I hate collegiate logic.

"There are exactly a hundred and fifty apartments in our building."

"I know," I reply. "You're looking at an ex-doorperson."

"Well then," he says, winding up to make some cockamamie point, and masculine-smug about it, "if somebody's husband cuts out in Walden Woods, don't you all hear about it, sooner or later?"

"Sooner, as a rule."

"Walden Woods and our building are communities of exactly the same size." He beams rather sweetly at this piece of clever validity. *So what's the big deal?* his eyes are asking.

"You see, Ed, I'd thought the one—compensation of being abandoned by my husband in New York was that at least I wouldn't be publicly embarrassed by it." His head's cocking, but I have no intention of being interrupted. "No, let me go on. For people of my background and conditioning and . . . er . . . generation, embarrassment is the big number. It encompasses rage, terror, despair, and any neurosis you care to name. In my . . . ah . . . day, marriage came with a lifetime guarantee—"

"You kidding?" he inquires, working gristle out between his front teeth, which are slightly spaced. "What about Elizabeth Taylor?"

I stretch out arms, presenting myself. "Is this—was this ever—Elizabeth Taylor? Let me go on. Marriage was supposed to be perfect and for life. It was more than a sacrament. It was a sure thing. And now that I find out it isn't, I'm profoundly embarrassed. By the way, Elizabeth Taylor is a lot older than I am. Twel—fif—I don't know. A completely different generation."

"Did you love him?"

"He isn't dead unless he's popped off very recently."

"Okay. Do you love him?"

"Not at the moment. But what I'm trying to tell you is that embarrassment has taken over completely." I allow myself a long look at Ed's square fingers circling on the tabletop, poking into my business.

"I'm just trying," he says, "to figure where your head's at now."

"Would you settle for befuddled?"

"Befuddled," he says, "doesn't cover going crazy on the carpet."

"Be good enough not to throw that in my face again."

"No, but to tell you the truth I think you're still pretty hung up on him."

How can you explain to a newborn the cumulative effect of sixteen years of marriage, or anything else?

"We were family to each other," I say. "I have lost a family member. I'm . . . grieved. That wasn't craziness on the carpet; that was keening and wailing."

"It's not death," he explains to me. "I mean, you could—theoretically speaking—just go back to . . . ah . . . wherever—Walden Woods and raise hell. You know. Make a stink. Get him back."

And while I'm hauling off to respond to this nonsense, I notice his eyes are appraising. He's testing me, gauging my response. I'm flattered and unnerved. I respond: "Now *that* really would be embarrassing." I narrowly escape saying, *What would the neighbors think?*, shuddering at the very thought.

"Couldn't you?" he challenges.

"Ed, I frankly don't see myself going back to club Tom over the head and drag him out of somebody else's cave. That is not an option. Besides, I'm in shock. I must do nothing till I hear from me."

"You had no forewarning at all? He just hauled ass?"

I nod.

"You guys didn't do a lot of fighting?"

"Only on the final night. And if we'd been habitual brawlers, I expect Grannie Elphinstone would have it all on tape. Besides, loud and uproarious slugfests are bad form where we come from. Domestic differences are negotiated by stinging retorts and lawyers. Even marriage counseling is thought showy. Also, my husband left me for another woman, which is really embarrassing."

"It's not as big a put-down as if he just left, without anybody else in the picture."

I hadn't thought of that. It probably would have been worse if Tom had preferred solitude to me. I concede the point but have to say, "And what qualifies you as such a—marriage maven?"

"Well," he begins, all confidence, "Hilda—my grandmother—was married a lot. I have an older sister whose divorce just came through. And then, of course, my parents were married. My dad died when I was in eighth grade. I'd like to think they'd have gone the distance, but in Scarsdale, you never know. . . ."

He lets his voice drift off into speculation. If he were only drier behind the ears, I'd suspect him of wryness. I begin to wonder which one of us is the more mature. Yet again I find myself disoriented.

We take the IRT local uptown. If you're going to hang out with the recently graduated, you can kiss cabs good-bye. We went dutch on dinner, and I bought my own subway token.

There are no seats on the train. Ed hangs from an overhead handle provided for the convenience of passengers over six feet tall in a city overrun with runts. I cling to his belt, staggering all the way.

We're parted at the noxious Fourteenth Street stop by a beggar who comes through the car on a dolly composed of plywood and rollerskates. The beggar has no legs, hips, nothing below the waist. He has insufficient body to support life, and yet he's parting the throng with aplomb, maintaining balance and moving right along in a car I can barely stand up in. For whole seconds I refuse to regard my own case as hopeless ever again.

We alight at 51st Street, in the autumn evening, stroll east toward the river. The sensation of returning from a first date is unmistakable. It takes me back. Way back. Nostalgia is beginning to sweep over me, but no, I can never leave a good mood alone.

"Say, listen, who'd you say that college roommate of yours was? The one from Mankato?"

He looks down at me. "Paulette Petersen. Why? You know her?"

"No. I was just verifying her gender."

Co-ed housing in all its depravity. This is what college life sank to after the SDS. Acid dropping like rain in an atmosphere hardly cleared of Mace. I picture joss sticks, candles puddling as in Sue-Jo Pennypacker Russo's bedroom, significantly stained mattresses reaching to every wall. "How convenient," is what I say.

"Not too," says Ed. "She was pinned to a fifteen-hundred-meter runner, and they were never out of the sack. I spent most of a term in the bathroom."

We pace off half the Summit Hotel's tasteless length. "Pinned?" I ask. "As in fraternity pin?"

He nods.

"You lived with this gir—woman, but her—ah—lover lived in a fraternity house?" I bog down in this melange of life-styles.

"Yeah. He was a Deke or something. Fraternities were making a comeback, but I was still a little too preppie for that scene."

"You, a preppie? As in *Love Story*?"

"Well, partial preppie—Scarsdale-modified preppie. Button-down broadcloth, docksiders, a certain amount of madras. Mostly just the look unless you were really serious about Princeton."

"Button-down broadcloth," I ponder. "You?"

"Yeah, except my sister kept stealing them."

"Getting back to your roommate. Was she attractive?"

"Sort of a Liv Ullmann type. Low-key Scandinavian. Not bad."

"You lived with this attractive girl, but there was nothing between you?"

"Well, like I say, the fifteen-hundred-meter runner was between us most of the time. Anyway, it was considered very uncool to get it on with your roommate. It led to hassles and a lot of room-switching midterm."

My mind has whirled back to the old Tri-Delt house, that fudge kitchen nunnery of Paleolithic times. "And the bathroom you spent most of a term in. It was a communal bathroom, for boys *and* g—men *and* women?"

"Wasn't supposed to be, but the women kept using ours because theirs was always crowded. And they were always busting in to see what a urinal looks like. It really blew them away, especially the ones who'd never been to France."

I've never seen one myself, and the whole concept strikes me as hilarious. "And this total experience of girls flaunting their lovers and giggling at your urinal and stealing your shirts hasn't soured you on women for life?"

"Why should it?" He looks mildly puzzled. "Of course that whole co-ed housing business was basically unworkable—left over, I guess, from—would it be the early seventies? Some time way back."

I cringe.

"But still, it had its points. Men and women live in the same world. After all, that's what marriage is all about, isn't it?"

Search me.

"At least I never had to go through that weird scene of buying corsages for the prom and filling out dance programs and whatever."

I cringe again. "You never . . . ah . . . got it on with Paulette?"

"Not till the last night of the term. And then only out of a combination of horniness on my part and curiosity on hers."

"And?"

His shoulders seem to rise upward into the night. "She married the runner."

This is not your regulation macho-menaced boy talking. But who is it?

We're approaching the bastions of home now. The doorman is fast asleep behind the grilled door and will take some rousing. "Getting back to the subject of bathrooms," Ed says on our way through the lobby, "it's too bad you don't feel like using your own tub because of that Mrs. Weillup thing."

We're interring ourselves in the coffin elevator. "I will learn to come to terms with it," I say directly into his chest.

Somehow, his hands are under my elbows, and they seem to be guiding me yet closer. The schooner of SoHo Heinekens has seemed to go to my head. I lurch forward, climbing his feet. The world goes athletic department T-shirt gray.

"What I meant was," Ed rumbles softly, "why don't you shower at my place?"

CHAPTER 13

AWAKE in a crepuscular dawn. The scene is Grannie Elphinstone's bedroom, and a muscular, hairy leg, not hers, lies heavily across my pelvis. Beyond the foot of Grannie's four-poster is Grannie herself—a photograph of her or possibly a tintype, prominent upon her dresser.

She's framed in pierced silver holding a fan like a truncheon and wearing wrought-iron lace. The portrait is Edwardian, and Grannie's vanished beauty is of the stronger sort. She appears to have just refreshed herself by wrestling Lillian Russell to the mat.

Her dresser top is eloquently biographical. Even pinned to the mattress, I can make out a wooden-handled curling iron, a ragged *Social Register*, a china hair receiver in the shape of Madame Pompadour, five simply framed photos of whipped-looking men in detachable collars, a duty-free flagon of Vol de Nuit, and a flattened tube of Preparation H.

The scent of Coty powder mingles with a nearer whiff of Desenex. With an eye as bold as Grannie's I follow the hairy leg up to its logical conjunction.

I have not slept with a twenty-three-year-old since the Johnson administration, and then only one. There's much I seem to have forgotten. The all-night nudity, for one thing—and how furiously the innocent sleep—and the being confused by a dozing bed partner for a puffy pillow to be set upon suddenly and pummeled into new shapes—his splayed posture at center bed, leaving the pummeled partner clinging to far edges, bolt awake. The sex parts are athletic. But the sleeping part between is a veritable track meet.

Nor is this the first night of the broad jump. I haven't sent one of my sensible nighties to the laundry in more than a month. I'm sleeping days again too. And such is the curative power of sudden sex that I'm showering—Mrs. Weillup be damned—in my own bathroom, sometimes alone.

Ed makes love with his glasses on, the better to see me, he says. My panicked response is to grapple wildly for the bedside lamps in vain attempts to pull plugs, break bulbs, anything. The result is I've knocked over both lamps at various times, cracking the glass tops on both of Grannie's bedside tables. Evidence, I have no doubt, that will be used against me.

The first fine rapture should be subsiding now and the guilt growing. But there's no sign of either on either side. I've had second thoughts, but always at the mirror—never in bed. Besides, I dare take none of this seriously. I must gather strength for the moment when Ed reverts to his generation.

How shall I recognize the end of the affair in time? And buffer my ragged emotions against it? I try even to foresee the final scene, as inevitable as Greek tragedy, when he strolls out of my life, skates over his shoulder, heading off for the Roxy Roller Disco. And I school myself in advance not to drop to the floor, howling and keening again, until he's cleared the door.

In the meantime I'm moving swiftly past prudery and only occasionally, while entwined, see the suddenly materialized face of Libby Smallwood peering aghast over Ed's plunging shoulder.

Tom's face I can hardly remember.

I've had to reorder my impression of the younger generation. My notion derives from the streets where they seem to have hardly enough energy to plant one sneaker in front of the other unless they're making off with your purse.

But this sweeping generalization hardly covers Ed, this blond Bucky Dent who will shortly arise aroused in the unforgiving light of dawn and then spring directly from me to Grannie's monitor-top refrigerator, where he'll quaff his "power drink," a blend of fruit, juices, lecithin, wheat germ, and kelp. I joined him one morning in a glass and spent an endlessly hectic day entirely in the bathroom.

But before he stirs, I'm at leisure to run through one of my recurring dawnmares. The one in which Grannie returns unheralded from Aiken to find her grandson in the sack with an old bag.

I take comfort in all the locks that range down her front door, especially the one with the drop-down iron bar. Surely even she isn't proof against all this hardware. And yet the geography of her apartment gives me pause. Over the years she's bought up the units of expired neighbors and has run at least three apartments together. What were once walk-in closets now lead to additional parlors. The bedroom where we lie meshed is directly beneath my living room and so was once a living room of its own. And the pullman kitchen beneath mine is indeed a wet bar, stocked with dusty cut crystal and the makings for power drink.

Grannie's decor runs to pesky small tables with peeling marquetry tops, three stages of soot-heavy curtains drooping before dead air conditioners, and row on row of books bought by the yard, in shelves flanking the Gothic mousehole fireplace.

Elsewhere in the endless estate sale of her warren I've counted two kitchens, three and a half baths, four rosewood sofas in splitting damask, a tapestry seeming to depict the castration of Abelard, a cedar closet full of fur stoles and winged insects, and a Tiffany lamp and a studio portrait of Alben W. Barkley, both signed.

The overall effect is of Madame Tussaud's basement level, and I dread the return of its principal waxwork.

Because upon her return I'll either have to surrender Ed to his own generation or move him upstairs to 6B. Either alternative seems—is—too momentous to contemplate at this hour. But my morning meditation has come to an end. My partner in crime is coming out of his coma. The first sign is unmistakable.

Despite my rapturous nights and stunned days, time moves on. Somewhere outside the windows that we steam up, New York is slouching toward winter. Santas are suiting up in the bowels of E. J. Korvette's, and the hookers on Lex are wearing leg-warmers. Both 6B and Grannie's lair are banked with brown, husky chrysanthemums that Ed has moved in from the roof for the winter.

But can I relax and enjoy this finite idyll? Can I even take wicked pleasure in this sudden surfeit of sex which surely I had coming to me? And how I'm being freed of inhibitions I didn't know I had?

Not entirely. A double-dozen puritan ancestresses leap at me from out of my lineage at odd moments, fling me down, work me over, shave my head once again for collaborating with the enemy.

And since I've given Tom grounds for divorce, I'm suddenly obsessed with legalities.

Now that lawyers advertise on TV, I've heard the term *no-fault divorce* and like its disinterested ring. Dressed as austerely as Wallis Warfield Simpson in the dock, I repair to the reference library at Fifth and 40th and miraculously find it open. This I take for a sign. It requires the whole staff to track down a definition of no-fault divorce and a volume on Illinois law. The more I learn of no-fault, the better it sounds: the quiet, unacrimonious termination of marriage a year after a mutual agreement.

But wouldn't you know it? Illinois has no no-fault. Just the old family favorites: adultery, impotence, insanity, attempted poisoning with intent, the infecting of one's partner with venereal disease. All of the above.

I wander tensely back up Madison Avenue, blind and deaf to the wiggling fingers and noisy puckerings of obese construction workers, my head awhirl with this laundry list of lurid grounds. Evidently I haven't been divorced behind my back, though why it matters I don't know, which also makes me tense.

This is one of our nights for dining at Watership Down. Our dining out is modest, ranging along the hamburgers-to-wheatgerm circuit. Monetary considerations aside, Ed owns no neckties. At Watership Down, balletic waiters with heavy, exotic heads drooping at the tops of slender stalks serve up haystack salads and macrobiotic quiche. We walk hand in hand along quiet side streets, and I hope we're not going to pass the theater that persists in showing *Harold and Maude*.

The high-tension wire in my arm is sending impulses to my clenched fist. "Relax," Ed says, once on the way and again at the table.

I have never been able to relax on command and say so.

"What's got you so strung out?"

"I'm O.D.-ing on bean curd."

"Be serious," he says, "but relaxed."

"I've been wondering all day if I'm divorced."

"Why not find out? Why not call your old man?"

"My *what*? Anyway, how would I put it? 'Say, listen, Tom, what's our marital status?' "

"Sounds good to me."

"You're not making the call. And what if *she* answered?"

"Then you wouldn't have to talk to him."

"I don't know their number."

"Don't you have a mutual friend or somebody?"

Libby looms suddenly above Ed's shoulder again. So used to seeing her in bed with us, I goggle at her ghost here in public. She's been more places with me than with Chuck. "I have a friend who would gladly tell me all about my private business, but I'd cut off my ear like Van Gogh before I'd listen to her."

"Then she's no friend."

How simple life is for the young.

"You don't want to know about this divorce business, do you?"

Yes. No. Maybe.

"And you want to know why?" He jabs at me with a celery stalk. "Subconsciously, you're waiting for him to come back."

"Ha," I say, considering this.

"You're waiting for him to come back, and then you two can sweep this whole thing under the rug and pretend it never happened."

"That's nonsense."

"It's the truth. Is your mother living?"

Good grief, how did she get into this conversation? "She was on Mother's Day. The card didn't come back."

"Where is she?"

She's down in Sun City hiding from bridge foursomes because she's the only one without a grandmother bracelet. "Arizona."

"Have you told her you and he aren't living together?"

One must leave *something* to say on a Christmas card. "No, I haven't, but then she and I don't swap girlish secrets. My not telling her is not—significant."

"Have you told anybody?"

"Not a living soul," I say, deciding to play into his hands. "Not even Isabelle Van Donder, who'd be amused."

"Who's she?"

"6D."

"You mean Mrs. Sternhagen?"

"Probably."

"How do you know her?"

How do you? "It's too complicated to explain."

"Know what I'd like to hear you say?" His blond brow is beetling, and I'd like to have both hands locked at the back of his neck and end this inquisition with hungry kisses.

"What?"

"That if he comes back, you'll kick his ass all the way down to the lobby."

He's looking earnest now, and his cornflower eyes are direct and undreamy. "What's in it for me?" I ask, coy as hell.

"Me." He stretches an arm across the table, his soil-seamed palm up, inviting my hand, demanding it.

I'm staring at quiche crumbs in my lap. "Don't say any more," I mumble. "You don't—"

"Oh, but I do. The kid's crazy about you."

I can't look the kid in the eye. "You know," I say, "we've been talking around this age business. I mean, I'm fif—twel—several years older than you are."

"So's Faye Dunaway." His tongue pops lewdly out, and he begins to make panting sounds.

"Leave her out of this."

"So's Charlotte Rampling (pant, pant)."

"Her too. One of these days you're going to want . . . somebody more your own age." It's a struggle, but I get it said.

"Every twenty-three-year-old woman I know majored in sociology at City, takes her laundry home, and talks too much about her father."

"I went through some of that," I reason. "You get over most of it."

"You're over it now."

"Yes, and when—something else is, well, not over, but . . . less important between us than it is now . . ."

"You talking sex?"

I incline my head.

"Well, when we get past the fucking-our-brains-out stage, we can settle down to a marriage of true minds."

"Keep your voice down. And where'd you hear that phrase?"

"What? Fu—"

"No. The other one. Marriage of true minds."

His eyes widen innocently. "Channel Thirteen?"

I sigh, gather my meager forces. "I think you've got me all wrong. If you're looking for an experienced woman, you're barking up the wrong girl. In all my years of marriage—sixteen, Ed, sixteen—in all those years, I learned nothing at all—zip. When my husband left me, I didn't even see it coming. You remember how I was—practically in traction. I'd been complacent, arrogant, and dumb as a post." I drop back in the chair.

"That's it," he says, as if I've just clinched the deal. "Can you picture a twenty-three-year-old woman admitting that she's complacent, arrogant, and dumb as a post? And they all are."

Of course I can't picture it. I can barely picture *me* saying it. But I'm almost positive that's not the point.

His hand is still lying palm up among the dishes. "Come on," he says, "put her there, partner."

I can't quite. It means something obscurely definite. My hand creeps to my edge of the table. I'm more skittish than all his coltish generation and can't help it. We've ordered frozen carob yogurt for dessert. A waiter who seems to be on point appears at my elbow. He slides the yogurt in front of me and bends. Warm breath from red lips gusts my nape. The waiter's muttering directly into my ear. "Listen, lady, if you don't want him . . ."

CHAPTER 14

ANOTHER crepuscular dawn and I'm jarred awake by some sound other than the knocking radiators. Ed lies crucified upon the bed, one leg hooked around one of mine. I'm working a kink out of my free knee and trying without luck to drag a sheet and a blanket up to our navels.

There are distant city noises—sanitation men Frisbeeing tin lids. But nearer there's a scraping within the walls, as of an enormous roach. Except roaches do not drop their keys.

I'm steadily more awake, instructing my hand to reach for the bedside lamp sprawling on its shade. But the hand lies frozen in gray sheets, wedding band glowing in the limp light.

The room seems to shudder. A crumb of plaster oozes

from the top of the bookcase and splatters near the miniature hearth. An earth tremor, perhaps, except only the bookcase moves.

Yes, the shelves are moving, casting a new shadow. The collected works of Vicki Baum begin to turn their spines my way. This is too gothic even for here. A secret door—the fire door, in fact—disguised as a bookcase? It begins to swing freer across the floor, edging a foot, two feet open. I yearn to reach for Ed with the unbiddable hand. Nothing. This is one of those nightmares in which the question of flight does not arise.

To add to the theatrics, red light from the fire stairs behind the bookcase washes the far corner of the room, and a shadow looms. A headless furry creature is edging by degrees into the room. Oh, if only Hieronymus Bosch were here and I were not.

I have not thought to scream, and still the shaggy thing bumbles farther into the room on invisible paws. But of course that red light isn't from the fire stairs. That's Hell's fire, and this is the Bear of God come to condemn sinners. It seems to be lumbering backward, bent in a ghastly crouch and dragging something behind it, a . . . a Vuitton suitcase on wheels.

It turns to the room, rises on its hind legs and becomes . . . who else? Mrs. Elphinstone.

She collapses against the bookcase, forcing it back into place with more than enough strength. Her hat, a cross between the Queen Mother's and Bella Abzug's, is askew, obscuring her view of the bedroom. She's clothed beneath the fur—a hardy Handmacher suit. In her arms is a great sheaf of flyaway autumn oak leaves, making her look like a vast ruined Finnish masseuse.

The room and I are growing brighter by the moment. The disguised fire door is her private entrance so that she can cir-

cumnavigate the locks on her front door. There's a certain
logic—twisted and hers—to the arrangement. And it's my
worst fear come true in a twinkling.

Still not noticing us, she speaks to the room at large, as
from a lectern. "Fortunately," she intones, "I got the number
of that cab driver."

And then: "I won't bathe until evening. What I need now
is six uninterrupted hours of sleep." She fights off her mink
and advances toward the bed.

In the last moment before I'm discovered, I manage to
twitch the corner of a sheet over Ed's crotch, missing my
own completely.

She throws the brim of her hat back, and it hangs from a
spike in her back hair. She sees me and her wattles sway.
The leaves drop.

In a rare moment of hesitation she glances quickly over her
shoulder back at the bookcase. Can she have overshot her
apartment by a floor and entered mine? No. Unlike me, she
has only moments of disorientation, not days. She skewers
me, all of me, with a stare. "Mrs. Renfrew, I believe?"

She cannot have believed it was Mr.

Ed, who can sleep through anything, is beginning to stir.
His grandmother watches as his hand moves up me and
closes over one of my frightened nipples.

"Edward!" she booms.

He's awake now—blinking at the room, up on his elbows,
his hand fallen away from my graven image. He heaves himself further up and the sheet slips free of his manhood.
"Hilda? Welcome home, sweetheart."

Grannie's—Hilda's old lips twitch. She's trying hard to
look past me and not too far down Ed. Her old hand, loose
with rings, waggles at him. "Edward, you naughty boy. And
both my tabletops cracked too."

I draw a veil over the seconds it took me to slip, bent double, past her and the many minutes I needed to find a sadly demure shirtwaist dress cast in the corner—the pantyhose I slung around my neck—the heeled sandal I finally found wedged under Hilda's wheeled valise—the bra I thrust into my purse, and the catch it jammed with padded cotton. And all this eternity, Ed with more poise than can be good for anybody engages his grandmother in studied, steady patter, leaving me free to flee. They let me go and chat on even as I throw all the bolts and work all the combinations on the front door locks.

Back up in 6B the first direct rays of November sun play across my horror. Convulsed with my old bugaboo, embarrassment, I burst into the bathroom and throw up copiously in the direction of the sink.

The phone rings its head off five times during the day, a record. I am at home to no one and sit through the hours fully clothed in a twin set like Libby's. Drawn up into a small space on the loveseat, I tuck legs beneath me and jam the skirt in all around. Prim too late.

I consider watching TV but then fear I may have made the noon news. And all escape is cut off. She's as liable to be in the elevator as on the fire stairs. I part the curtains and stare down at the street, where every passerby seems to be looking up and pointing at my window. By midafternoon, I'm scarcely human.

At four o'clock, someone knocks on my door. I flinch and drag a curtain back again, wondering if the ledge outside will hold me. The knocking goes on: methodical, confident. Whoever's out there is sure to have a key. I walk the last mile to the door and throw it open.

She's in the hall, towering over me. I've never seen her without her furs, and she's bigger without them. Still in her traveling suit and with both hands on her hips. The great tree trunks of her legs burgeon down to boat-sized carpet slippers. "Oh, for heaven's sake," she explodes, "come down and have tea. Barbara, isn't it? Don't be a fool!"

I follow in her wake. Has my life any other direction?

We have tea in one of her dining rooms I have never discovered. The table is Market-Crash Mission. The breakfront has breasts. She pours out from a pot rainbowed with tarnish.

Since she can't be bothered with small talk, there's no buildup beyond the offering of a cracked plate of Peek Freans. I don't trust a saucer in my hands, but she sits back from the table and nestles her tea into her front. The dainty souvenir spoon she stirs with is lost in her grip.

"You're not worried about *me*?" she barks suddenly, thrusting the great public monument of her face over the cup. "Don't be. I have outlived all my enemies and can afford to be mellow. Heavens! I'd rather see a woman in your situation doing *something*. Just look at Isabelle Sternhagen. She's gone completely to seed."

In silence we think our various thoughts about the seediness of 6D.

"You were quite right," she goes on, "not to have him at your place. One can't be too careful of one's reputation until the divorce comes through. Yours hasn't, I take it."

I tell her I don't know in an impotent little voice I've never heard before.

"Quite right too." She nods, endlessly agreeable. "It doesn't do to look too eager until a divorce is final. It only means the settlement has to be done over.

"My granddaughter, little Madeline—Ed's older sister—has just gone through a divorce, and she's done awfully well out of it. Have you met her?

"No? Well, you must. You won't find us an intrusive family; we're Protestants, both sides, right back to Jamestown.

Little Madeline's mother—Ed's too, of course—is a bit Scarsdale for my taste. I have never cared for the suburbs. I'd
rather make my own rules. Don't worry about her. I don't."

I clear my throat, looking for my tongue. "Actually, I suppose I am a sort of . . . interlude in his life."

She plops her saucer onto the table and shows interest at
my first complete sentence. "Really? I think he's a perfect
darling, don't you?"

"World Class," I bleat, softer than before.

"Well, then, if you're fond of him, I wouldn't worry about
things from his viewpoint. Apart from the fact that it's
always the woman who decides, he's not the love-'em-and-
leave-'em kind. I wouldn't hear of that. With that kind of
life, they always finish up picking someone at random.
They're restless from variety and then find they've been
served leftovers in the end. And by leftovers, I don't mean
second time around. I mean *leftovers*."

I thread my way through the jungle of her logic, looking
for a clearing. "I'm too old for him," I blurt, and idiot tears
sting my eyes.

"Are you?" The genial old horror leans closer. Her glasses
are round mirrors framed in folded flesh. She runs a crumb-
chasing tongue under her lower plate. "At my age everybody
looks young. Of course you're looking a little drawn today,
but I'm not seeing you at your best, am I?"

"Not even near."

"How old are you?"

I writhe.

"Never mind. I can peg you within six months. I know all
about it; I was forty-seven for twenty years. And men ought
to marry older women. That way you have a far better
chance of coming out even. This country *stinks* of widows.
Look at me and be warned; all my husbands are probably

dead by now. And don't tell me people don't marry any more. Never have so many married so often."

I'm whole thoughts behind her, but still she plunges on like a cart horse. "And consider the precedents: Agatha Christie, Lillie Langtry, Mrs. Patrick Campbell, Mrs. Harding. I know most of them personally. And Lady Randolph Churchill, if you please. She married two men younger than her *sons*. And don't forget Raymond Chandler's wife. She snatched him from the cradle and died in his arms."

She settles back, snug among her arguments, and sucks at her tea. I await the clincher, which is: "And never think that Edward is looking for a mother. He already has one, as you're bound to find out."

I come away from Hilda Elphinstone unassuaged. All that charity might be malice directed toward her daughter-in-law if it isn't outright madness. Back in 6B I throw up again, as copiously as before.

It's morning again, and Ed is awake before me—a first. He's propped up in bed, and it's mine. Affectionate as he and Hilda are, he moved in with me on the evening of her return. Wordlessly he homed in on the emptied drawers in my deserted bedroom. The cavities that once cradled sincere socks are stacked now in plaid flannel and athletic department gray. There appear to be two sorts of men in the world: the boxer-shorted and the Jockey-briefed. I have had one of each. There's also power drink in my refrigerator, and I've tripped twice over a trowel. I've even run my slender repertoire of dinner menus past him, and not even this has driven him into the night. The young talk knowledgeably about nutrition and eat anything.

He's propped up against the headboard, a recumbent Elgin marble. His glasses are on—are they ever off? And he's got a clipboard on his knees, sketching the diagram of an herb garden rockery on graph paper. In a lower quadrant he letters: BABY'S BREATH.

The bed seems to be in motion. I'm groggy, bilious, and for some reason literary. I gesture broadly at a pie-shaped planting in his rockery. " 'There's rosemary, that's for remembrance . . .' " I quote.

"It needs dappled shade," he says, deep in thought, far from Hamlet, whose indecisiveness would leave him cold. "What did you and Hilda•talk about?"

She seems to be offering your hand in marriage, I do not say. "Mrs. Raymond Chandler," I do say, "Mrs. Patrick Campbell."

"I haven't met any of those Aiken people," he says, preoccupied again.

The bed's pitching like a porch swing now, and I think of asking him why he doesn't notice, but my throat's full. I reach for my robe and snag it on the third swipe. I make it to the bathroom with seconds to spare, though it's uphill both going and coming back.

He's heard my gurgling regurgitations and the growling gags and then the denouement of dry heaves. His knees are still sheeted and the clipboard's still in place, but the cap is on his pen. He regards me with Hilda's own all-seeing gaze. "Let me look at your breasts," he says.

"Oh, you animal," I wheeze, wedged against the canting doorframe, "not now."

"Come on," he says, smoothing a place beside him in the sheets with a clinical hand. I settle there just as the bed swoops my way. He opens the top of my robe. "They're browner, aren't they?"

"What are?" I say as in a dream.

His hand cups a light burden. His thumb skims a nipple. "And they're more sensitive, aren't they?"

"Ouch," I say distantly.

"Barbara—"

"How do you know so much?"

"I took a course—Changing Role of the Male in the Matrix of the Marriage Dynamic—two-hour elective."

"Where's my calendar?" I inquire, the sea rising around me.

"You don't need a calendar, Barbara," he says softly, the clinical hand caressing, "just *think*, Barbara."

Oh, Barbara, just think.   •

CHAPTER 15

'VE found a gynecologist. And like all gynecologists around here, his office is tucked beneath a brownstone stoop, where he's clearly hiding from the AMA. My already puffing ankles descend behind a row of garbage cans into the former coal bin of his outer office. The receptionist, a balding strawberry blonde, seems to be having a hot flash.

As I enter, she drops an emery board and turns her flushed, angry face to the typewriter. "Oi yam bus-y," she chants adenoidally into her keyboard. "Siddown," she adds, or possibly, "giddout."

I turn to the room. In a far corner nestled in a plastic sofa is a young woman nine months gone, with ankles like eggplants and full breasts aimed all over the room. She shakes her head quickly. I turn back to Blondie and hold my ground, staring holes into the empty typewriter roller.

She turns with slow menace for a look at my waistline. This is our nearest brush with eye contact. "You a patient?"

"I am willing to be."

"Because Doctor don't take new patients." She looks pointedly past me to the door. In her glasses are the sockets of rhinestones. "Who sent ya?"

"Circumstances."

She sighs. "You're gonna hafta do better than that. You recommended by one of Doctor's patients? Because—"

"I recommend her," comes a sudden voice from the corner.

Blondie's head bobs around me and sends a death ray to the dim corner. "You don't even know her, *Miss* Proctor."

I turn to the kindly eggplant person. "Hello," she pipes as if we're in the room alone. "My name's Polly Proctor."

Outnumbered, bully Blondie reaches for her appointment book. "Doctor can see you in January."

"I'll wait," I say, "here."

Polly chortles. She wears a sort of Day-Glo disco tent over what must be a multiple birth. "Come and sit here. He'll see you after me. If he was that busy, he'd be on Park."

The phone rings, saving Blondie's face. It's the first of four calls for Doctor: two from his broker and two more regarding resort real estate. Apparently one is about to have one's pelvis examined by a cartel.

"It's not that he isn't competent, exactly," Polly muses. "His bedside manner's for shit, but then who's isn't? I've thought it might be his glasses. They reflect."

We devise a routine of speaking to each other only when Blondie's tied up on the phone. It drives her bughouse. Nodding toward her, I say, "What's the story on the charm-school flunkout?"

"It's his wife," Polly mouths elaborately. "Wait till you see his *nurse*." Roly-poly Polly rocks with laughter. "I've got to watch myself. My water could go like any minute. You here for a Pap, or is this the big number?"

I tell her I have a feeling it's the latter.

"How late are you?"

"Enough," I sigh.

"How—"

The phone crashes down on its cradle. Blondie, fiery red, finds her tongue. "Who the hell you think you are," she fires at Polly, "the Doctor?"

"Doctor Proctor!" Polly wheezes, grabbing at her sides. "Oh, don't let me laugh. I got a bladder like a used condom. How long you been married?" she asks, pressing on regardless.

"Ah . . . sixteen years, but . . . sixteen years."

"Oh, wow, I sense a story in this." Polly nudges me. "I did temporary typing at *Newsweek*. Go with it."

What have I got to lose? I've uncovered the only good listener in New York. I explain to receptive Polly that I'm not living with my husband.

"Some other dude?" she beams.

I nod, oddly proud.

"You plan this?" She points at my belt.

"I haven't had a plan in my head for months."

"Got any other kids? No? Let me get a handle on this," Polly ponders. "You been married sixteen years, but the minute you get it on with some other stud, it's vomit time?"

She has summed things up.

"Sort of puts the old ball in your husband's court, doesn't it?"

She has an odd way with words, but effective. All those Walden Woods years I spent feeling subconsciously like a spayed cat, and . . . could it be I'd been sleeping the whole time with a low sperm count? I savor this theory that's obliquely disloyal to Tom. The more I think of it, the likelier it is. I might well have thought of it before, but I've been so *busy*.

Distracted, I miss the first part of Polly's history. "—Third one I started," she's saying, "but I just said to myself, what the heck, why not have it? Decision-wise, it's major, but I'm rent-stabilized. And I'm going to raise it on my own. The father's gay. He says he really wants it, but you know how it'd be every Saturday night. I'd be down under the Westside Highway with a flashlight. So I says to him, look, get off my back and I'll tell your mother you're the father. Like it'll really help his image with her, you know? And everybody's happy. With food stamps, free-lance, and unemployment, I figure—"

A door opens and something in starched white that could mark your baby crooks a finger at Polly. It's the nurse, and I recognize her at once. She's Grace Poole from *Jane Eyre*.

Between the two of us, we get Polly on her feet. She gives me the thumbs up sign and walks widely into the examina-tion room, another ship passing in the New York night.

And to think I hesitated telling her my little story.

Grace has me stripped, sheeted, and in the saddle. Doctor approaches and she passes him what seems to be a tray of stainless steel hors d'oeuvres.

He looks like a corrupt Keebler elf and goes to work on me at eye level without stooping. He's tiny everywhere but in the finger.

And lest I seduce him from the stirrups, Grace is never out of reach. With unexpected flair she does wonderful Sally Rand things with the sheets, revealing me in a peek-a-boo here, a flash of flesh there. We could set it to music.

Doctor's all over me in jig time while some mental meter ticks away the exorbitant minutes. Somehow I gather I'll be paying in cash.

Doctor's glasses are roughly the thickness of Aldous Huxley's. And as Polly says, they reflect. I keep catching awesome, science-fictional glimpses of my nether self. Weird, hairy, pink shots that seem arty photography of something unpleasantly exotic: a tendriled sea anemone, perhaps.

Afterward, in a scene out of a Russian customs shed, Grace watches me dress. She points me to an office more inner still, farther from windows.

Doctor is shrugging even as I enter. I wonder as I so often wonder about New Yorkers what he *really* wanted to do with his life. "How can I know till we hear from the lab?" he asks petulantly, turning small palms and long fingers up. "But you've got one in the oven, if you ask me."

If I ask him?

He warms to the topic somewhat and makes little jabs with a gold pen on my fresh new record. He underscores my age with many lines and delivers a whole sermonette on amniocentesis.

My mind recoils from the promise of a hypodermic probing like his glittering pen into the hot aquarium of my womb. The distinct possibility of a punctured placenta. The odds on infection. The potential for premature labor. The needle that can graze—enter even—the veined eggshell dome of the—

Enough. My ears close until his chair pushes back. He seems to be standing. "There's risk involved," he's saying. "Would I lie to you? But at your age . . . Besides, you want a perfect baby, doncha?"

Yes. "Yes." Suddenly, more than anything, ever.

I tread carefully away from Doctor, climbing curbs with exaggerated care, looking both ways before crossing one-way streets. I seem to be walking for two.

The sidewalk is a narrowing corridor lined both sides with

shoulder-high garbage in bursting bags. We're having a strike by the sanitation men. No, we've had that one. This one's a strike by the garbage scow crews. All these deadly spray cans, these empty Entenmann's boxes, these cardboard suitcases stuffed with the corpses of household pets, should be adrift in an Atlantic sealane. I fear infection on every hand, consider trying to walk with my legs crossed.

But, no. Somewhere inside me—and, no, I don't have to wait two days to hear from the lab; I know. Somewhere inside me is an embryonic Manhattanite. Minuscule now, but already unfurling small fins, reaching for his city, immune to everything. And soon—oh, how many months? You count back and then you count forward and then—and soon I'll be wheeling him—him? in a stroller looking for a park and a whiff of green. But this hardy little Dead End Kid will breathe anything, take his first step in anything, be—the mind boggles—a native New Yorker. He won't be born; he'll merely elbow me out of the way.

I'm smiling now and crying and walking with the strict attention of the stoned, and a delivery boy on a skateboard gives me a wide berth.

I weep euphorically to the very door of 6B, laughing all the way.

I hardly know the place. It's never looked much better than Motel 6, but who could be house-proud here? Now I view Mrs. Weillup's fiber glass curtains with alarm: the pinch pleats drooping from missing pins along the dime store rod. The rug beige at the periphery and gray down the middle. And can I get a crib into the bedroom? The nesting instinct hits me like a blunt instrument at the base of the skull.

I've forgotten to take off my coat, sit down, make coffee, do whatever you do when you come home. I'm standing in the near night, one elbow on the Welsh dresser, rhapsodizing about Pampers. A key turns in the front door. I could take it off its hinges and put the crib out by the elevator for all the privacy I get around here.

He steps up behind me, smelling faintly of potting soil. His hands circle my waist, come to rest on my stomach. From habit I inhale to simulate svelte. But then I let go, hang out, bulge. . . .

"Well?" He nuzzles my neck, brushes my ear with his lips, enfolds me.

"I wish I smoked so I could quit."

"The lab tests?"

"Forty-eight hours, but . . ."

"You know. Turn around."

"I don't . . ."

"What?"

"I don't have to have it."

His arms go rigid. It's not even what I meant to say, and I wish I hadn't, but I have.

I can feel the hurt even in his hands. "Why would you say something like that?" he wonders.

Why indeed? "Because I'm thirty-eight years old is why, and when this baby graduates from college, I'll be *sixty*." And then I sob, which probably saves the moment.

He turns me around and I step on my foot. His eyes are enormous behind the lenses, faking profound shock. "Thirty-eight! And all this time I thought you were just a hard-living twenty." His thumb searches my neck for chins. Square, not-clean fingers massage my temples for elongated crows-feet. He checks out my forehead for furrows. His hands drop to my navel, groping for drooping breasts.

"Stop it," I say faintly.

"Thirty-eight," he repeats, shaking his head. "You finally got it said, and it wasn't so hard, was it?"

"Yes, it was."

"You have your little hang-ups, don't you, like telling your age and saying, 'I love you, Ed.' "

"You know it wouldn't work. I could . . . you wouldn't have to . . . I could have the baby and take care of it myself. That's a major concession. We don't do that sort of thing in Walden Woods. But I could be one of those crisp business-women who can find housekeepers. Polly Proctor's going to raise hers. I mean it's a completely different situation, but . . . You could go on being . . ."

"A legal minor?"

"Why should you be tied down? There must be things you want to do."

"There are." He's easing me to the floor. Somehow we're crumpling slowly without bumping knees or sprawling or anything.

"Look," he's saying, busy with my belt, "I'm not Dennis Hopper, and I'm not Peter Fonda. That was a really old movie. I don't want to take off on my bike for Ash-Haight-bury."

"Haight-Ashbury."

"Whatever. Listen, when they were having Woodstock, or whatever it was, I was a Trekkie playing Pop Warner foot-ball."

"I missed all that myself," I say. "So they had a revolution and neither of us came. Is that anything to build on?"

"If it is, let's go with it. You've got me confused with some other whole scene. All I can remember is one recession after another. I'd like a little security."

"I've lived so long, the generations are beginning to blend," I sigh. "And you see the problem yourself. When-ever anything went wrong between us, I'd blame it on your age. We'd use our ages against each other. It'd be like a mixed marriage."

It occurs to me too late that only his grandmother and I have ever mentioned marriage.

He's peeling autumn taupe nylon off me now, and I'm not making it difficult. We get to the ankles. "Take your shoes off," he says, pulling his shirt over his head without dislodging his glasses. "When you're sixty, I'll do all this for you. Strip you naked, splay you on the bed, and hump away like you're not even in the room. You can just lie there with your teeth in a glass, and you won't know I'm there."

"Oh, that's so repulsive," I murmur.

"Did you know you can get a fungus from wearing pantyhose all the time? You've got to let your whole body breathe. Seriously."

There's no reasoning with him. "Do you know what gives you away?" I say on my back, unbuttoning my blouse. "You think you know everything. It's—callow. When you're a little older—"

"Come on. Off with the bra too. I'm not the gynecologist. I want to see everything at once."

"How do you *know* things like that, you . . . twerp."

"Did he tell you we can do this up till about three weeks before the baby comes, later even?" He flings his jeans all over the loveseat. "We can. I think by then you have to lie on your side and stick your leg up in the air, and then I get around here and—"

"Oh, shut up, Ed."

"What's that?" He peers over my shoulder. The floor's excruciating, and I'm between a rock and a . . . hard place. And something I've been wearing is wadded in the small of my back.

"How's that again, lady? Did I hear you say, 'I love you, Ed'?"

"No, you didn't."

Somehow the backs of my knees have gotten hooked over

his shoulders. Most of my weight is distributed at the top of my spine, and I'm half airborne, beginning to fly. His head drops between my ever-spreading knees, and his ear flattens against my stomach.

"Hear that?" he says to the occupant of my uterus. "Are you getting this?" he inquires of the next generation. "Do you hear Daddy crying out for love and Mommy calling him callow twerp? This is some start in life, right? And where does it leave you, kid?"

"Please," I moan, though I'd be moaning anyway, "please, not in front of the child."

CHAPTER 16

THE telephone voice is tinny but recognizable—Blondie's. Bernice by name and somewhat softened from our earlier encounter. They've heard from the lab, and before she puts me through to Doctor, she wants to know if I want this baby.

"Yes." I'm laughing, freaking out, whooping it up. "Yes, certainly. Been waiting for this for years."

It's possible I was and didn't know it. The possibilities are limitless. So are the years, practically.

She puts me on hold while she conveys my mood to Doctor.

He comes on, nearly civil with congratulations. We calculate it'll be a July birth, while I visualize the midnight flit in the hard-to-find cab through steaming streets perilous with the switchblades of summer and exploding manhole covers. *(Labor room and step on it.)* Doctor and I make another date.

My date book is filling up. Though I'd like nothing better than to curl up someplace and try to give everything serious thought, this is the day Ed has decreed I'm to meet his sister.

I have no doubt that what we have here is in the nature of a commitment. This is his next logical step after speaking directly to a fetus. He means to outnumber me, bulldoze me with superior forces. Breach my defenses, blitz my principal cities, cut off my supply routes and avenues of retreat. How I struggle against the entreaties of this *Playgirl* foldout. Can life become more complicated than this? Yes, and I'm coming to that part now.

For the sister encounter we decide on the cocktail hour. I'll show up at her place alone and he'll follow after work. If I've got to meet her at all, something about arriving on his arm seems all wrong. Grotesque, even.

The way to her address takes me down 53rd past a shop called Modern Mater. I lose myself and five minutes staring at a display window completely filled by a mannequin in a youthful maternity mode. A real Polly Proctor number with scooped neck and falling folds in fire-engine red matte jersey. Strange emotions war in my breast. I move on to Madeline's.

She's seemed to do very well out of her divorce. Her building is the Excelsior. The shop off the lobby sells Rolls-Royces. I'm bowed over terrazzo by much gold braid and personally conducted thirty floors up in the elevator by an extrovert in a Cossack's costume. "You want *Mrs.* Wilkinson?" he says, confirming, "because *Mr.* Wilkinson is down on five now. Mrs. Wilkinson kept the view."

Good for her, I do not say.

Her door is opening as I approach, trying not to waddle. Behind her willowy silhouette the view beyond the living room encompasses all Manhattan and far out to sea. I can just make out Shannon Airport.

"Barbara," she says, extending a hand that turns palm up in the air. She's wearing pants over four-inch heels, an egg-shell sweater under a braided Mary McFadden belt. She has hair the color of Ed's, anchored on top with a barrette, not plastic. I try to place her type and can't quite. In school voting, she was probably a shoo-in for Best All-Around.

"I've been looking forward to this." Her tone is pleasantly insinuating. "Really." She's behind me now, sweeping off my coat.

We turn for a first confrontation. Her gaze swoops down to monitor my midsection. Oh, yes, she knows. They all know. Mayor Koch knows.

At least she's not intimidatingly young. There's a hint of graininess under the eye liner. We're not going to have to talk Kiss concerts or find dead-serious social commentary underlying *Saturday Night Live*. There's no heavy hint of Hilda Elphinstone about her either, not even a preview. "Now call me Madeline, for heaven's sake."

She leads the way deeper into the room, over much pale parquet and superior sisal. "And will they let you drink?"

Speaking to her back, I'm bold as brass. "Do you know I'm going to have a baby? . . . Madeline?"

She whirls around, clasps hands before her cleavage, makes a steeple of her fingers. "Yes." She nods elaborately.

"But—"

"Ed called your doctor and then me."

Yes, yes, outnumbered already.

"And I'm tickled to death," she says, "really. Are you?"

In some odd way, tickled to death may even be about right. I settle into a chair. "A small sherry," I say in a small voice.

She laughs deep in her throat. "You sound like Hilda. It's always a small sherry with her too, but I've seen her kill the bottle. God, I hope I'm still knocking them back at her age. She's marvelous, isn't she?"

I agree to the general opinion.

She goes for the drinks. Unlike mine, the kitchen is a room unto itself. I scan the living room, which is done in High Conran's. A lot of polished pine and softly satirical London-between-the wars upholstery. The lamps are faintly industrial, and there's a mammoth Lowell Nesbitt iris unframed along the longest wall.

She's back, settling opposite me, urging her chair an inch closer. We're going to be cordial if it kills me. She hoists her glass on high. "Well, what shall we drink to?"

We ponder. "World's oldest unwed mother?" I propose.

She pulls a long face but keeps it light. "I think Ed has plans about that." She winks brightly.

"Technically," I say, "I'm married already."

She waves this superfluous information away with a hand still wearing a wedding band.

"I married right out of college," I blunder on.

"Oh, so did I," she chimes in. "Sarah Lawrence. I didn't even finish.

"And then that first shock of finding myself single nearly freaked me out. Of course I had Ed to back me up, but then so do you."

I'm still nodding.

"They say men mature more slowly than we do, but really Ed knows who he is already. And what he wants."

I keep nodding. I might as well. "I don't know why he wants me," I say, easing my guard down. Way down.

"I do." She's a New Yorker. She knows everything. "He wants a finished product. You're good for him. He's always been so *impatient* with young girls. I'd meet each one precisely once, and then—oblivion. When his brother-in-law was still around, he used to drool over them all like mad. He's down on—"

"Five," I say.

She nods. "Probably with one of Ed's rejects if I know him. A real male *nympho*. Honestly, I got so I could hardly stand the sight of him." She goes for the sherry bottle and comes back. I'm just going to have one more.

"It's all so ridiculous and . . . undignified," I say, beginning to roll. "And this baby forces the issue. How can I think? What's happened to all the free choices we're supposed to have these days? I feel like Phyllis Schlafly at an orgy." I gesture broadly and slop sherry. "I barely hinted at not going on with this pregnancy—"

"Oh, you didn't, did you? Ed's such an idealist."

"I know. I know. Every time I open my mouth, I want to call for a translator. What kind of a basis for a relationship is that? You talk about the generation gap—and now I've got another one on the way." I point unnecessarily toward my navel.

I'm really cranking up now: "I've gotten through whole epochs of modern history by hiding out in Walden Woods and keeping a very low emotional profile in a serviceable marriage. And now I feel as if I've been hit by a truck."

"With Ed at the wheel." Madeline smiles. "You've let yourself get totally hassled by side issues, haven't you?"

Easy for her to talk. Maybe I have, and why not? Life has more loose threads than an Ohrbach's knockoff. I slip out of my shoes.

"Leaving all the difficulties out of it for a minute," she says, tracing a fingertip around the top of her glass, "what do you want?"

My eyes grow shifty, but there's no retreat. My supply trains are on sidings somewhere, blazing merrily. "There are days when I want to be back in a suburban center-hall colonial, watching everybody age uniformly."

"Seriously though."

I know. I've known all along, or for days at least.

"I want—I can't say it. You remember how *The Graduate* ends. He's going to take a walk one of these days, and I don't want to have . . . wanted anything."

She gazes far out to sea, a rebuke to my short-sightedness. "He won't, you know. He's steady as a rock. And *very* pigheaded. Be glad you're in love with him. If you weren't, he'd be an awful pest. You are, aren't you?"

She knows I am. I'm perilously near simpering but have to say, "That he's caught me on the rebound hardly expresses it. When he marched into my life, I was still in emotional traction. He caught me—"

"You aren't actually going to say he caught you with your pants down, are you?"

Actually, I was.

Her eyes are huge, and she's rollicking with silent, conspiring laughter, and she's slipped out of her shoes, maybe to keep me company. One shoe falls my way, and I can read the label in the instep from here. Maud Frizon. She's done beautifully out of this divorce.

The room's hermetically sealed. The only distant sound is a Piedmont flight looking for LaGuardia.

"What I really want," I tell her in all candor, "is to hold him in my arms without clinging for as long as it lasts. Preferably forever." My voice wobbles toward the end.

She thinks. Looks at me and away. Runs a rosy-tipped index finger down the line of her neck. "I don't blame you," she says, quiet and unbrittle. "I know exactly how you feel." A key turns in the door.

It opens behind me, and Madeline's eyes light up. I shift around and see Ed in the doorway, pea-jacketed, chukkabooted, grinning widely. Something's attached to his hand. He enters the room and draws something—another hand in with him. It's a girl: hip-high boots, designer jeans, sheepskin coat open over a golf shirt laundered to the correct shade of red. Though annoyingly anorectic, she's a dazzling blonde with a knowing grin. There are grins all around. I go blind from the glare.

"There you two are." Madeline rises. The room seems thronged. I make it out of the chair in two stages without grunting, the sherry singing in my ears.

"Hi, Mom," Ed says, approaching, and I blush or flash hot or something. "How'd you two get along?"

"Old friends," Madeline says, taking his chin in both hands and kissing him on the forehead.

"Isn't anybody going to introduce me?" says Miss Anorexia. Ed draws her into our circle. "Barbara, this is my sister, Madeline."

Her hand is out. Mine isn't. "What?" I blurt.

There's a moment of complete silence, rather like death.

"Oh, dear," says the imposter with the sherry glass, "you mean, you thought . . ." She can hardly meet my glazed stare.

"I mean," she babbles, "the minute I heard you and little Madeline were meeting, I dashed down from Scarsdale and told her to take a walk or go to Bloomingdale's or someplace so we could get acquainted. Oh, my dear, I'm not his sister. I'm his mother."

CHAPTER 17

"DON'T touch me. I've never been so humiliated in my life. 'Big Madeline.' 'Little Madeline.' They sound like the two principal inmates of a whorehouse."

It's long past dark, and Ed's led me, chattering with rage and cold, to that little riverfront park below the 59th Street Bridge. All its lights are a-twinkle, and I know he's picked it for its romantic associations with Woody Allen's *Manhattan*, and I'm not buying. Besides, the effect was ruined in advance. To get here we had to walk past the rummage store run by Planned Parenthood.

"Why didn't you *tell* me your mother's name is Madeline too?"

He shrugs, like Doctor. "I just didn't think about it. I've always called her Mom."

"I don't know why. You call your grandmother Hilda."

"Actually, she's not my grandmother; she's my great-grandmother. There's a generation missing in there."

"I wish they all were."

"Calling somebody Great-grandmother sounds a little—awkward."

"And I suppose what I've just been through *isn't*? Oh, put your arms around me. I'm freezing. I thought I'd known embarrassment before, but it took you and your—oh, what's the use? I don't even want to talk to you."

He's trying his level best to look abashed. "I thought—I mean how could you think she was my sister? Scarsdale sticks out all over her. Couldn't you see that?"

"I can now, and a fat lot of good it does me. I could die. They must be laughing their heads off, the b—"

"Hey, don't." He lays a cold hand on my hot cheek. "Don't." He moves my chin with his thumb, finds my lips with his to still my ranting. I go a little weak in the knees from habit.

But as soon as my lips are free, they're moving. "She led me on. I'm sure of it. She's vicious. If I could just remember exactly what she said—"

"Look, before you knew who she was, did you like her?"

"Now that I think about it . . . Oh, well, yes, I suppose. *Naturally* we got along all right. We're practically contemporaries. She can't possibly be more than ten years older than—"

"Eight," he says, "actually."

"What a comfort you are. And Little Madeline, your much-vaunted older sister?"

"About twenty months older than me."

I sigh. Sob. Shudder. "Why *wouldn't* I like them? And Hilda too. They're practically giving you out like a door prize. It's unnatural. Even if the whole thing was . . . suitable, I'd expect the women in your family to put up at least a little bit of a fight, but, oh, no, not them. Butter wouldn't melt in their mouths. They're like a goddamn King Family special."

He gathers me up, flattening my cheek against his chest, pulling my heels out of my shoes. "Basically," I say in a blurred voice, gearing down, "I'm mad at myself. If I'd ever let myself think about your mother, I'd have pictured somebody more—League-of-Women-Voters. I was so quick to see her as your sister. It sort of bridged the gap between you and me, fool that I was. Oh, what a horse's ass I've made out of myself."

I whimper. He rocks me back and forth, like a . . . baby. "You want to know why Mom and Madeline and Hilda didn't make things rough for you?"

"Because they've all spoiled you rotten and always let you have anything you wanted?"

"Maybe," he says, maddeningly reasonable. "And maybe because they respect me and what I want. Because I'm the man in the family, and they need a man around. Don't you?"

He turns me and I ease back into my shoes. We're going to try brisk walks now. At the first intersection I still want to hail a cab I can throw myself under. "Don't you?" he repeats.

I could be crying now, hard, on general principles. "I don't know. I'm so *confused*."

"That's what I love about you," he says. "You're so bitchin' vulnerable."

"I wasn't before I knew you."

"Yes, you were," says Mr. Know-It-All. "You always were."

We're heading down Sutton Place before I speak again.

Bulletproof Lincolns with reading lamps sigh into portes co-
chères. We pace the long row of superior doormen. In a voice
I invite the wind to catch, I say, "I love you, Ed."

He hardly reacts beyond tucking my head more tightly
into his armpit. "That's my girl," he says.

Girl.

We go to a back table at Joe Burns for supper, where
we're cursed with the only attentive waitress in New York.
She's fleet of foot and eighteen inches of waist and seems to
be an out-of-work hoofer of the To-Dance-Is-to-Live school.
She refills Ed's coffee cup at roughly twice the rate of mine.

He's given way to boyish euphoria, and we clasp hands
amid the cutlery. "So tell me the truth," he's saying. "Would
you say you loved me even if I hadn't knocked you up?"

Miraculously, the waitress is back for this. She squeals.
She's brought us more butter, though we finished eating
some while ago. She hovers back into the near distance.

"Fool," I murmur, "of course I love you. Who doesn't? *She*
loves you." I jerk my head at the waitress. It almost sum-
mons her. "But, Ed, you've got to realize that people don't
marry every last person they love."

"You have, haven't you? Up till me?"

The conversation begins to describe loops, which may run
in his family. "If you mean did I love Tom when I married
him and was he my first—everything, yes, of course I loved
him. It was senior year."

"What does that mean?"

"I have no idea and refuse to be held responsible. I was
somebody else then. And in fifteen years you'll be somebody
else too."

He's shaking his head. "Whoever I'll be, I'll be with you.
We'd better make it legal. I'd like another one."

The waitress materializes. She thinks he means coffee.

"I'd like another baby," he says, "after this one."

The waitress squeals.

I nearly join her.

"Ed, listen to me. I'll do well to have this one." I really am pretty near the end of my rope. It's been one of those days.

His euphoria's gone now. He grips my hands, engulfs me with his eyes. "You're not worried, are you? About the amniocentesis and all."

I gape. "How can you know about all that? Did the doctor tell you?"

"No. I asked him."

"Is this something else you picked up in that Matrix of Marriage class?"

He smiles confidently.

"Ed, marriage is not a minicourse."

"Right. We can get fifty years out of ours—easy. And when you're dead, they're going to chisel a big smiling face on your tombstone."

"Oh, that's so depressing. Talking about my tombstone at a time like this."

Yes, the waitress is back for this too. And she turns a concerned gaze on Ed. On Ed, not me. She tops off his coffee and recedes reluctantly.

"But the good thing about amniocentesis is," he's saying, "we'll know the baby's sex ahead of time. Then we can work out the name and know what color to paint everything."

"But do you really know about babies? Oh, yes, I'm sure you do. But let me remind you that they're loud, they smell, and they're terribly expensive." I've contrived to turn a baby into a British sportscar without dampening his mood. Beaming, he calls for the check, which is placed directly into his hand.

But he doesn't get paid till tomorrow. Luckily, I have a twenty and change in my purse, though I have to dig for it.

The waitress is half across the table, walling me out. "I guess," she breathes to Ed, "people are always saying how much you look like John Denver."

"Far out," Ed says obediently. "The . . . ah . . . lady is paying."

He's still bubbling with plans out on the sidewalk. But for my condition, we'd be racing down the middle of First Avenue, scarves snapping, as in one of those emphysema-defying cigarette ads.

"You'd better get in touch with your husband," he says, working down a mental roster, "and get the divorce business squared away." He manages to make it sound automatic, like after-hours banking. "And then—"

"Ed, I really don't think I can go through with any of this. Don't get your—"

"But you said—"

"I know what I said."

"You didn't say why, though."

"Why what?" I'm getting lost again.

"Why you love me."

"Let me count the ways," I say, knowing full well quotations don't work with him. "I love you because on the day when New York finally falls completely apart, you'll be out there at dawn piling one stone on top of another, creating . . . dappled shade—and order—and hope. And it'd be wonderful to be on your side because you're—brand new and cocksure and simplistic, and for whole minutes you make me feel that way too, and it's irresistible, but I think with a little basic self-discipline I'll be able to resist.

"And besides, everytime I look at you, my heart turns over, and if that ever happened to me before, I can't remember it." I run down.

"Well," he says, apparently impressed, "those are great reasons. So you'll marry me, won't you?"

Fatigue washes over me. "And what are we going to live on?" I brace for the single word *love*.

"Hilda," he says. "At first. Then I'm due for a raise early next year, and then we can—"

"Ed, don't." Griffins skulk in the darkness. The grilled front door throws barred light across the sidewalk.

"You will, won't you?" He draws me back from the light, and his hands begin their moves. I can't let him and my nerve endings gang up on me again. I inhale deep drafts of cold, questionable air.

"I've got to think all this out. Let me do it. Don't plan. Don't think about the future or anything else. Just give me some time."

We walk into the lobby, somehow separate. The doorman attempts to tell me something across an unbreachable language barrier. In the elevator we're necessarily thrown together again. We kiss with care, and the light touch brings me nearer the brink than he knows. Unless he really does know everything.

The elevator grinds to the fifth floor halt. I've pushed Hilda's floor as well as my own. "Go stay with her tonight." I put an urging hand on his arm. "Give me a night alone."

"But—"

"I need it."

The doors begin to close, and he's outside. His mouth forms *marry me*.

Gently I reply, "John Denver, my ass." And then I'm looking at badly aligned metal, and the elevator climbs up one more floor.

On six, I think seriously of pushing five again but don't. Between the elevator and 6B, I drop my keys and listen to the echo. How gladly I've forgotten what being alone at night is like. In the forty-watt gloom, I can't tell one key from another. Visions of shadows in ski masks crouching in stairwells will themselves into being. Rummaging for my keys in a city where half the citizenry is out on bail, I hazard a look over my shoulder at an infinity of blank doors dwindling into the distance.

Six B's door starts to open and closes again, which it always does if you don't start with the bolt key. I begin again in proper sequence. The door swings open, and I must have left the overhead light on in the foyer.

I think of coffee, but my eyelids are already nailed open. I think of hot chocolate and gag. The living room radiator is hammering out tribal rhythms. I stand in the foyer still trying to convince myself about the overhead light.

The bedroom door is slightly ajar. I go into the bathroom, throw off my clothes, and climb into the Weillup Memorial Tub, letting tepid water lap me up. In the tall tier of bathrooms, toilets flush plaintively far above, and somebody groans in his sleep.

I float like my own child and calibrate the rising curve between my hipbones. I'm somewhere beyond tired, staggering toward exhaustion. I drift, and a small voice near my inner ear simpers, *Now call me Madeline, for heaven's sake.*

I lie in this limbo until I'm sure I can sleep, then pull the plug with my toes.

Dead on my feet I mistake the bathmat for a towel and rub myself all over with rubber-backed shag. Reaching for the robe that is never on the hook behind the door, I find it isn't and sarong myself with a towel.

In the darkened bedroom, I make for the closet, stumble over a suitcase just inside, and find my robe, though what I want is a nightgown. But I'll wear the robe to bed; the heat's off for the night. And why did I trip over that suitcase? My suitcase is downstairs in the storeroom.

I'm awake again, utterly.

I turn—slowly, slowly—in the darkened room. There's a man in my bed.

He's lying face down on top of the bedspread, fully clothed. A dark suit, with one white hand dangling down and white fingers curled on the Boukhara.

His feet at the end of the bed—in shoes, or are those dark socks?—aren't six inches from me. Dear God, not another dead body. My hand is over my mouth, and I'm screaming down my throat. He turns onto his back. His mouth's a black circle. He begins to snore. My hands and the robe drop.

Tom's back.

CHAPTER 18

GO groping all over the wall, looking for the light switch. He swallows in midsnore, snuffles, reaches with an automatic hand for the knot on his hardly loosened tie. The room floods with light.

He's wearing a three-piece suit. His wing tips are lined up on the floor. He sits up, and despite gray hair spikey in the light, he looks as young as—he looks very young.

Working the heel of a hand into one eye, he squints at me. "Barbara?" he presumes. He scans my sarong. I hope he doesn't think for one minute I took off my clothes *after* I discovered him. But men will think in the most self-congratulatory terms possible.

"Get up, Tom."

In my last memory of him, he was slumped on this very

bed, maundering about Marlene Millsap. Will I find her in the living room, catching a rerun of *The Odd Couple*?

I go for my robe, and he throws his legs over the edge of the bed. There's a moment of silent scrambling which my faltering brain fails to use.

"I must have dozed off," he says in a voice oddly familiar. "Where have you been?"

Is this an accusation? I jerk a bow in the sash of the robe he gave me two birthdays ago. Besides, to explain where I've been would run to three volumes. "Out."

I begin to see already. We're to regard the missing months just past as something on the order of a delayed commuter train. "I am often out," I say. Not that often, really. At about this hour I'm usually to be found right there in that bed, naked as a jaybird, with—

"I grabbed a plane that was due in at nine, but we were on the ground at O'Hare for an hour and a half—fog."

Lucky I didn't sent a Fugazi limo out to pick him up.

"I ate on the plane," he adds.

My hands are on my hips in the classic termagant posture. "Care to tell me what you're doing here?"

He plays for time by searching for his shoes.

"Don't put those on," I say, "and don't clump around. There are—people downstairs."

"Could we have . . . coffee?"

I give him my back and stalk very lightly out of the room. In the kitchenette I fling freeze-dried instant into cups and put the kettle on. He's suddenly behind me. "What in the hell is all that stuff in my dresser drawers?"

Oh . . . that.

He's holding a wadded sweatshirt, the one emblazoned SCARSDALE LACROSSE, but he appears not to have read it.

"Don't unpack," I say. "You're not staying."

He has entered my drawers for the last time.

"Let's wait for the coffee." Suddenly chastened he retreats to the bedroom, perhaps to rifle it for more clues. Wait till he finds the sack of Weed-N-Feed behind the vacuum.

My head's pounding and whirling. *Search for Tomorrow* could get six weeks out of my last half day. And didn't I know he'd be back? No, I didn't. I've come to believe implicitly in Marlene Millsap without even thinking about her.

The watched kettle boils almost at once. This scene is destined to run at top speed, without time for reflection. I put the cups on a civilized tray. He settles on the loveseat, and his socked foot covers the place where my screaming head once flooded the carpet. I edge onto the chair.

It's possible that he means to drink the whole cup before speaking. Maybe ask for a refill. "Where's Marlene?" I query.

"She's in Madison."

I show no interest.

"Wisconsin."

Still no flicker from my side.

"She has a son there, at the university. You know him?"

I shake my head.

"Little creep they call Sonny. He was caught selling PCP."

Silence from me.

"Angel dust, I think it's called. It's a tranquilizer for wild animals. The kids mix it with marijuana and smoke it. He was making a fortune."

No value judgments from my side. Anyhow, scholarships are almost impossible for the middle class.

"She's gone up there because the university's threatening to hand him over to the local authorities."

I break my silence. "Where's Hube?"

"Her husband?"

"You tell me."

"He's in São Paulo. Brazil. Caterpillar transferred him."

And where are you in her hour of need? I avoid asking.

He puts his cup down on the floor next to an embalmed chrysanthemum. I'd forgotten the cleft in his chin that only shows up in shadow. He's making a business out of being sure the cup doesn't fall over.

He plants his hands on his legs. Far-reaching basketball fingers cover his kneecaps. There isn't a wrinkled pinstripe in his slept-in pants. He tries for a relaxed pose.

"Marlene has a daughter too," he says. "You know? Honey?"

"I beg your pardon."

"They call her Honey," he explains.

Sonny and Honey. How unfortunate.

"I left her home alone. Told her to go to her grandmother in Berwyn, but I doubt if she did. She won't have anything to do with me. Hates her mother too. She's fifteen." He shakes his head, attempting a deprecatory smile. "Kids are a pain in the ass."

Surely if that's anybody's line, it's mine.

"Barbara," he begins, "I—"

"Are Marlene and Hube divorced?"

His hands slip inward, meet between his knees, clasp. "As a matter of fact, yes. Hube got a divorce in South America. Or on the way. Haiti, I think it was. It's *ex parte*."

Ex parte, and all I know is no-fault. "Meaning?"

"It's a so-so divorce as far as it goes. It can't be challenged within its jurisdiction."

"You mean he's a free man only in Haiti?"

"It's not that shaky, but—"

"Is it quick?" I inquire—steely, legalistic.

"In and out. Same day. Look, Barbara—"

"Are you and Marlene married?"

He flinches, and not from me. "Married? Jesus Christ, Barbara, I'm married to you."

I stretch a hand in front of me and examine my nails. It's stagey, and I couldn't care less. "Are you sure?"

"Goddamn it, Barb—"

"You didn't used to use that kind of language," I say, distant now. "Life with Marlene and Honey must be a locker room. How do you know we aren't divorced? *Ex parte* for the goose is *ex parte* for the gander."

He looks at the ceiling. "You never even heard of *ex parte* before."

"No, but now that I have, I'm interested."

"Look, Barbara, I know you're hurt. I—"

"Do I look hurt?" I fold my arms across my middle.

He looks away, into the fireplace. "You look—great."

Yes, it's going to be difficult.

"You always looked great to me."

"Let's not start the trip down memory lane, Tom. If we do, you'll find yourself in a room at the Beekman Tower Hotel even sooner."

"Hey," he says, "I live here."

I'm shaking my head.

"In a lot of ways, I never left. I know I should have written, but—"

"No," I say, seeming to soothe, "you shouldn't have. At first, it would have been painful. Later, it wouldn't have mattered."

He runs his hand through close-cropped hair. "Barbara, if you'll just hear me out."

"I'd rather see you out."

"Please."

I've already examined my nails. I just sit there.

"Barbara, guys my age—"

Oh, no, not that.

"Guys my age . . . It's a syndrome. It happens. I tried to explain it to you before. You sit there at that goddamn—that office desk, and you don't even know how long. You take root. You think you've just been to your fifth college reunion and it's your fifteenth. And you look up one day, and here's this whole new crop of guys—young kids with brand new MBA's and moustaches and perpetual hard-ons—"

At the office?

"—And you're not one of them. You thought you were, and then you know you aren't. And it begins." His voice cracks.

"Why Marlene?"

I'd thought it tended to be cocktail waitresses, airline stewardesses. I seem to recall suspicions about the typing pool.

"What?"

"Mar-lene," I articulate.

"I honestly don't know. And now after a couple of months of her—"

Three and a half that I know of.

"—I think I must have been crazy. Some kind of actually clinical thing. She's really sort of a pig. And she drinks."

With Sonny and Honey, who wouldn't? "Careful," I say, "you'll have me on her side, and then where will you be?"

"Where am I now?" He speaks through a cage of his fingers.

"You're too late."

Two cars collide down at the corner. Otherwise, silence.

"Are you sure?" he says. "Be sure."

"I wasn't when I walked in here tonight. I am now."

He inclines my way without moving. "Can't we—"

"No."

"Can't we just look at it like a—a season out of our lives? A sabbatical?" He's a drowning man and it occurs to him. "Do you remember the night I told you—about Marlene?"

Clearly. "Faintly."

"I said we never tried hard enough. I shouldn't have said that. *I* didn't try hard enough." He taps his vest with an accusing finger. "I will now. I'll make it up to you."

"You can't."

"You used to be a little tough," he says, "but not like this, not hard."

"I'm not hard and I wasn't tough. I'm vulnerable and I always was. I have it on the best authority."

"Okay. Whatever you say." He reaches, lunges almost, and grasps my hands. They lie inert in his. "Let's go home," he says. His eyes crinkle. He'd wrinkle his nose at me except that would be going too far. He's groveling now, or very near. And I swear to God I'm not enjoying it.

"I'm already home," I say. "You're not."

"You can't mean you like New York." He gives my hands an extra squeeze. "This hole. It's no good for you."

"It was good enough to leave me in."

"I was only thinking about myself then. Now I'm only thinking about you."

"No," I say. "You haven't really gotten around to me yet. Maybe you'd better not."

"I've got an idea," he says as if he's just thought of it. "Let's go back. Not Walden Woods. But Wilmette, maybe. Or Lake Shore Drive. You like apartment living? We could get an apartment on the Drive. Or Astor Street. A big rambling place."

I think of an apartment, a real rambler. The one beneath our feet. With Hilda sprawled in her four-poster, and Ed somewhere else in the maze of mad rooms on some daybed with one leg thrown out over lavender-scented, unaired linen sheets. I think of Ed, and his baby stirs—in me.

I know it's too early for the baby to stir, but who said anything about an ordinary baby? This is little Mr. Gifted. Or Miss. I mean to be an insufferable mother. And I want to think about all that now, and not this.

I stand up. There's a pleasing ache throbbing in the region of my lower spine. I plant a maternal hand in the small of my back. Tom's finally on his feet, far, far above me.

"Go to Haiti, Tom."

"What? No. Listen, Bar—"

"Either you go or I go."

"Think what you're saying. You don't—"

"And why not go back to Marlene. You could do worse. There was a time when you thought you had. She could use you. I can't. You haven't burned that bridge. She doesn't even know you're gone yet, does she?"

He runs the back of his hand across his chin, and he can't look at me. "No. She doesn't."

I've talked him to the foyer now. "You might need me one of these days," he says, without malice.

"You could be right. I might. But by then it'll be too late. Don't forget your suitcase. And your shoes. Did you have a coat?"

"Chrissakes, Barbara, it's two thirty in the morning."

"New York never shuts down," I say. "I've had some good times at two thirty in the morning."

"You wouldn't set foot outside at this time of night."

"I never said I had."

He's at the door now, topcoat over his shoulder, suitcase in hand, wingtips, untied, on feet.

"They wonder about you back home. What's happened to you. What you're doing." He reaches out and touches my ear. I'd forgotten how he used to do that a long time ago, sometimes even when he was just going off to work.

"Tell them I'm shacked up with a twenty-three-year-old

kid and pregnant with his baby, but it's okay because his great-grandmother approves of me."

"Sure. Fine. Listen, about that Haiti business. If it's what you really want, then . . . okay. But let's give it some time. Let's wait a while until we're both sure."

"I'll give you a week," I say, reasonable, not tough, not hard. "And if I don't hear from you, I'll be on a plane myself to wherever it is: Port-au-Prince."

He starts away, out toward the elevator, and then turns back, which is the price I pay for not banging the door on him at once.

I can't help remembering the night behind the white pillars with the lights flashing curfew when he took his letter sweater off and draped it around my angora shoulders. There have been troths less tenderly plighted. I'd kiss him good-bye, but that would only lead to complications. But what's one more? I rise on my toes, and kiss him . . . off.

He knows exactly what it means. "I'm sorry," he says, "about everything."

I could comfort him now. I could comfort the whole world. This is Earth Mother speaking and I'm not even confused anymore. "Don't be sorry," I say. "I'm not. I wouldn't have changed a thing."

CHAPTER 19

CLASS NOTES
by
Your Faithful Scribe, Liz Welty Oberholtzer

Still a few Wedding Bells tinkling for the irrepressible Class of '65.

*Barbara Renfew (Blakely) (ΔΔΔ) and Edward Kimbell (Cornell, '80). Is this a misprint? Way to go, Barbie!

*Tom Renfrew (Sigma Chi and memorable varsity center) and Marlene Novak Millsap (Wright Junior College, '65).

CHRISTMASTIME weddings both, and though I can't speak for Tom and Marlene's, the keynote of ours was simplicity. I wore an ancient blue suit from Stanley Korshak with a straining waistband. Ed wore a new pair of corduroy pants, his Harris tweed sport coat, and a tie-less button-down broadcloth he borrowed back from little Madeline. My something borrowed was a ring that will do as a wedding band, a circlet of dim sapphires that Hilda said Mayor James J. Walker once gave her.

I'd thought City Hall would be nice. Ed, whose college electives never ran to Comparative Religions, thought St. Patrick's Cathedral. We settled for a small Murray Hill church of an ambiguously optimistic creed. The minister, who was into body jewelry and needlepoint kneelers, wanted to do a little premarital counseling, but our case defeated him. And he looked a little queasy when Ed told him all about amniocentesis.

I'm not willing to belabor the subject myself except to say that on a day even more wondrous than this one I learned that my baby is a flawless male, raring to go full term and well worth having.

And so on one bright December afternoon halfway through life, I found myself carrying one boy and marrying another. I promised to love, honor, and never in a fit of pique to tell Ed to grow up. And he promised to love, honor, and emboldened by the lab results, get me pregnant again at his first opportunity, and mine. Or words to that effect.

My only attendant was little Madeline, who appeared in what she'd worn Christmas shopping that morning. I haven't quite forgiven her for not being her mother, and she hasn't quite quit snickering every time she looks my way, but we're going to come to terms in time.

Big Madeline thought a sort of combined wedding reception and holiday open house at her Scarsdale place for eighty of her intimates would be nice, but majority opinion overruled her without my having to play the . . . heavy.

We gather after the ceremony at the Excelsior apartment for quiche from Eclair and champagne. A wedding cake too, which cheeky little Madeline has had festooned with rosettes of blue icing spelling out IT'S A BOY, which would hardly have played very well in Scarsdale.

She even lets Mr. Wilkinson, her ex, come up from the fifth floor just this once, and he stares undrooling at me. Big Madeline comes in and on like Dina Merrill. As we brush cheeks, I strike a bargain with her. If she'll scratch our first meeting from the record, I will never call her Mother Kimbell. She looks shaken and agreeable.

Hilda's there, with an umbrella on a cloudless day that doubles as a cane. In the modernity of little Madeline's apartment, she looks like a Mayan diety in a desert. And for a wedding present she's given us two tickets to London and a suite at the Dorchester. She was impatient when Ed explained he had no vacation time coming and incredulous that neither of us has a passport.

On her third glass of champagne she's still brooding. I settle beside her and she grips my hand suddenly. "My dear, you must always keep a valid passport. In '28 I took the Graf Zeppelin, quite on the spur of the moment." She looks across the distance between her world and ours, and there's pity in her old eyes.

When Ed and I are back in 6B, which is still mine, pending, he hands me a check Hilda gave him in lieu of London. It's for three thousand dollars.

My hand is less steady than hers. "Ed, we can't take that kind of money from her."

"Why not?" He's closing our suitcase for the weekend honeymoon. Then he turns with a look about the eyes that's noticeably older than the moment before. "You're right," he says. "You give it back to her."

Come next summer, it should divide about evenly between Doctor and the Harkness Pavilion, with enough left over for cabfare.

*   *   *

My honeymoon is not rife with the surprises of the Victorian bride's, but I'm astonished before we even leave town. At the Avis counter where we've reserved a car, Ed slides the contract my way. "And they'll need your driver's license."

"You don't mean," I say, amply within earshot of the beauty queen behind the counter, "that you can't drive?"

He turns both palms outward and devastates me with his eyes.

"No American boy—oh, never mind." I plunge around in my purse and come up with an Illinois license, still valid.

"At Scarsdale High School," he stage-whispers in my ear while I'm trying to fill out forms, "only the greasers had wheels."

The Avis lady, who is of course Brooke Shields thinly veiled, squeals. "Scarsdale High School?" She tweaks her darling little neck scarf in the company colors. "I went there!"

"No kidding," Ed says. "Who'd you have for social studies?"

So it begins.

The Connecticut inn we've chosen is run by a genial couple who are about our ages in reverse. Once the rest of the clientele, who seem to be Seventh Avenue garment men bedding down with out-of-town buyers, leave, we settle with the couple before the lobby hearth with mugs of hot buttered rum.

I manage to steer Ed away from expanding to strangers on amniocentesis, which may be of particular fascination to him because it wasn't performed on him. And, oh, what fun he's going to have timing contractions. And the female innkeeper seems not to have gone to high school with him or roomed with him in college, so we have a pleasant, nattering, bibulous evening. Ed tells the male innkeeper a trick or two for espaliering fruit trees and making potted poinsettias last. On my fourth mug I confide blearily to our hostess that we're on our honeymoon.

"Honestly?" she says. "I don't know *when* we've had a married couple."

Ed not only carries me over the threshold; he's carried me three flights up from the lobby, where I fall fast asleep in midsentence. He gives the bedroom door a gentle kick behind us, kisses my half-open eyes, and says, "Just leave your teeth in the glass. I'll do the rest."

The breakfast room is drafty, with views through holly wreaths to a frozen gray pond beyond. Ed leaves the table to take a call from New York.

It's from Miss Mapes in 7D. She's trying to contact both Madelines too. Hilda's been taken to the hospital. A stroke is suspected, and she's refusing treatment by the Third World doctors on call in the emergency room.

We start back at once, I hunched over the wheel the slick, serpentine length of the Hutchinson River Parkway, Ed silent, drumming his fingers on the dashboard. Glancing up once out across the colorless, uncomforting vista of the Maple Moor golf course.

Hilda is in a peeling green private room. She seems to have flunked intensive care, and they've banished her to this Pinesol-smelling outpost where she'll be no trouble to anybody. And here she sleeps mostly, in a minimum of flexible tubing, the line of her mouth drawn down on one side.

We set up a roster for sitting with her, I overlapping in the late afternoon with one Madeline or the other before Ed comes in for the evening. And when two or three of us are there together, we talk in subdued sickroom tones, wondering if she's asleep or listening.

Alone with her, I long to read every line in her face. Her profile is, if anything, stronger in repose, more honed and hawklike. One hand, a plastic ID bracelet at the wrist, lies exposed, with the wide-grooved nails gone ivory with age. And yet it's still full and unspotted, capable, and more restless than the rest of her.

She stirs occasionally, drinks from an angled glass straw, wakes up completely, sometimes in the present, sometimes in another era.

Once, when I'm lost in thought about the possibility of getting a job before the baby comes, she says perfectly clearly, "It's to be a boy, didn't they say? Yes. That would have been my idea entirely. We need more boys."

When I think of an answer, she's asleep again, her mouth drawn down more than before.

And then again she's awake, looking full at me. "Charlotte?" she says.

I am willing to be deputized for a missing generation, or anybody. "Yes?"

"You are not. Don't humor me. Go home now for a while. You have a marriage to see to."

When she sees I'm not inclined to leave, her hand sketches the faintest gesture of dismissal. "Go, girl," she says. "When I wake up, one of the Madelines will be here. It is like entertaining at an endless reception. Don't wear me out completely."

I go home, to her apartment. From our first night back, Ed has wanted us to live in her place, though we dress in mine. We are continually fussing with locks and rising and falling in the elevator. We rattle round two floors, probably the only two people in Manhattan with space to spare.

I arrive home at dusk, ready to pull together dinner in one of Hilda's incredible kitchens. Ed's sitting motionless in the nearest parlor: gilded youth against a dim rococo backdrop. He starts up to embrace me but then only pats the velvet cushion beside him on the camelback sofa. Dust billows up, and I settle next to him.

"I can't take it," he says, looking into his clasped hands. That staring at long, laced fingers is so like Tom that my heart falters. I think he means marriage, of course.

"I don't want her to go." I see there are tears in his blond lashes, refusing to fall. He means Hilda. I want to cradle him in my arms, but that's too—maternal. Instead, I run a hand along his jeaned thigh that comes to rest on his knee. That seems more right: part mother, part lover.

He looks at me through his round, owl lenses. "What if you hadn't married me?" he wants to know.

Quite clearly he means that the impending loss of this ninety-year-old-plus woman would be unendurable for him without me at his side. I start to tell him that life would go on for him without me and then see no reason for saying any such thing.

We gaze around the room. The accumulation of Hilda's things and years is her living presence, which is why he's insisted on staying here—staking it out, holding on to her. He runs an arm around me, gathering me in, the man in him mastering the small scared boy.

"It's not a downer for you, is it?" he asks. "Being here in her place."

Alben Barkley smiles thinly, yellowly from his frame. I notice for the first time a whole king's ransom of early pewter at the top of an armoire, webbed to the ceiling. A roach appears suddenly atop a beveled mirror and waves companionable antennae at us from across the room and the evolutionary experience.

"I would live in a cave with you," I say, and I mean it.

He enfolds me and we cradle one another, rocking the generation yet unborn. We sit there, married and unmoving, until night falls and the lamps that are never out in this parlor glow pink through irreplaceable silk and art glass. Only then does he ask me the eternal question: "What's for dinner?"

At the hospital the next evening I'm at my post, looking for signs of change in Hilda's face. I'm almost certain that I'm in the room alone when she says abruptly, "Get my glasses."

She waits while I turn out a drawer and fail to find them. But she takes the intention for the completed act. "There, that's better." She blinks in the gloom.

"We should really do this room over," she says, whether in jest or confusion I will never know.

Time skips a beat. "Make sure," she says distinctly, "that we have a six-month supply of soap, gasoline, and light bulbs. Other people call it *hoarding*. They can call it what they like."

As she drifts off, I wonder which of history's crises she has just confronted, if she's really looking back at all and not planning for the future.

Occasionally a nurse strays in by mistake, and by the second week Hilda's ordering her around like a servant she must have had. If the nurse is black, she calls her "Leonie" and her mouth twitches with shared jokes more private than she knows.

After hours of silence, she says, "Madeline," and I'm willing to be either of those if I can get away with it, but she goes on: "Madeline—little Madeline is to have all my bits and pieces of jewelry. Except for the sapphire ring. You keep that. And if she wants to sell everything, then let her. Fashions change. And for heaven's sake don't bury me in any of it. Those Egyptians . . ." She seems to be drifting off again, but I'm tired of letting her go.

"Hilda, what did you do to get that ring from Mayor Walker?"

Her eyes are open and darting my way. "I was to invite him to a weekend house party he had no intention of coming to and then swear later, if need be, that he'd been there." She purses half her mouth. "And so I earned it." One eye twinkles. "It was honestly come by." She sleeps again, exhausted and refreshed.

Not noting the hour that passes, she goes on. "You and Edward are to have my apartment, and everything in it. The Tiffany lamp alone is . . . but sell what you don't want. See the people at Parke-Bernet. Fashions—"

"Hilda, don't bother about—"

"It's no bother. I sent for the lawyer about all this the week before you and Edward were married. I saw this coming."

She would have, of course.

Perhaps a day, possibly two, go by in silence, but then she was never one for small talk, and she's changed as little as she can. And then she surprises herself into speech. "Oh, the times we had!" she says fervently, just back from somewhere. "And when we had to pay, we paid gladly. And I don't mean money."

And then: "Who are you?"

I keep preparing for her not to know, but still she does. "I mean you, Barbara. Who are you. Where did you come from?"

I search for an answer. "It would all sound so dull to you, Hilda."

Her tongue searches her mouth for the teeth that aren't there. "Well, life is dull now, isn't it? There aren't enough *opinions* somehow. And people live such little lives, don't they? And keep quiet. And put up with anything. And everyone's so *earnest*. I wouldn't want much more of that, not a minute. But I wouldn't change a minute past. Be able to say that on *your* deathbed, my dear."

And then she dies, not an arm's length from me.

Dull light in lines falls through the window blinds, across the floor, across the bed. I sit there with her for the hour before Ed comes, not reaching out to her, not pushing the bell that might bring a nurse. I mourn this old stranger-lady, and the baby does stir in me. And I yearn toward her wisdom and smile at the nonsense all her years make of our little differences.

And when Ed comes, he'll find us here just like this. And I'll think of the words to comfort him, and the ways.